D1784003

OUT THERE

by Daniel Schlordt

for my nanny,

thank you.

Meet The Family

It had been a long time dark. We had been driving for what felt like days along the winding roads, often single file, through the glens of Scotland. Sunlight peeped through the vast overhang of fir trees that filled the landscape like a cheeky child at bedtime. I had tried to pass the time with a crossword on the back of the newspaper I'd picked up from the petrol station when we filled the car, but I became increasingly nauseous with each twist or turn in the road. Then, at last, there was a clearing ahead, and like a flick of a switch, the car and road were engulfed in a booming vista of mountainous greens and an everlasting façade of land.

Mike gave a sharp, befuddled snort, which reminded me of his presence, something I perhaps should not have disregarded, considering he was driving the car. I looked at him and stared at him, but he showed no willingness to disclose a reason for his alarm. Likewise, I showed no sign of willingness to ascertain such information and instead turned to my left and stared out the window, watching the fields run past me. Three months had passed, and in that time, I couldn't remember when a conversation between Mike and I had more than as many words. This trip is our last chance. I reminded myself. After seven years of marriage and, in particular, the past three months of what can only be described as a living hell, we gave ourselves an ultimatum: to be together at the end of this weekend or to be apart.

-

As Graham navigated the car smoothly up the winding road and our country playlist kept us company, I felt overwhelmed.

"This is just my favourite time of year!" I exclaimed with a watery eye.

"I know, my love." Graham gently replied.

It had been three months since we'd all been together and all I wanted to do was forget that time - I couldn't wait to have my family together and put the past behind us. Every year since they left home, we always met somewhere for our anniversary. The location was different every year, and slowly, new family members joined. Mike was first after he married Claire, Steven was second, and Jackson joined us for the first time only last year, but of course, this year's new addition in the back seat of our car is little Rubeus: who had slept the entire journey from Moffat.

We'd chosen a lodge hidden high up in the Scottish glens after I felt last year's city break to Manchester was too busy. I just want to spend concentrated time with my family; they're all I have at the end of the day. Plus, we had to have somewhere suitable for my little man to join us.

"Rubeus is still sleeping. He has been an absolute gem." Graham assured me as he noticed I was struggling in my attempts to see him in the backseat in my visor mirror.

\-

"Kyle, your mum and that bloody dog! She's just sent a selfie with it in the car's back seat."

"I know! You'd think she'd never had kids." I jokingly replied.

"Ellie has seen it but hasn't replied. That will rile your mum...."

I loved this drive and felt good about the weekend. Both Steven and I loved the countryside, and after his first week in his promotion at work, he needed this break; plus, the icing on the cake came only this morning when we found out we were officially on the waiting list to adopt a baby.

"Kyle..." Steven exhaled with a majestic tone.

"Steven..." I replied, matching his intonation.

"Can you imagine driving to wherever your mum decides next year and sending her a selfie with our baby in the back?"

"Stop! I'm trying not to think about it. I don't want to upset Claire this weekend. She and Mike are having serious issues."

"I get that, I do. But maybe our good news will help Claire get over what happened. I also think she sometimes forgets that Mike is grieving too."

"Oh well, no one can be as perfect as us! I just want to see how the weekend goes and how certain people feel before telling everyone. I don't want to waste our good news when certain people won't appreciate it."

I am happy. Extremely happy. Content even. I am excited for the weekend, I've always loved our family trips, and it's not come soon enough for our family. I watch the hills cascade around my perfect man and me as we edge further into nowhere.

-

I notice Jackson smirking in my peripheral vision and can't help but smile too. Mum has been on the phone for a solid ten minutes giving me a hard time for not replying to her photo on the family chat. She's banging on about feelings, and all I can do to stop myself from laughing is a grunt in acknowledgement. But then, she starts breaking up, and I believe there might actually be a god for a moment. I catch her saying she's a few miles away just before we get cut off. I'm surprised we've even got signal way out here.

"Your mum?" Jackson asks knowingly.

"How did you know? What on earth gave it away? Could it have been my exhaustion with her?"

"Ellie, your mum just likes the reassurance of responses."

"And I like not giving her the reassurance of responses!"

Jackson lets out a disapproving sigh, and I can see his eyebrow raised as he flicks between staring at the road and the car's navigation system.

"I hope Claire is OK this weekend," I state, changing the subject. "She and Mike really do deserve this break. I just hope she doesn't drag down the atmosphere. She'll make mum feel sad, which will make Kyle sad, and it's just too much sadness!"

"I know. This weekend is always about your mum and dad thought, so I doubt Claire would take that away from them. I doubt Mike would let her - "

"LET HER!?"

"You know what I mean, Ellie!"

"Am I allowed to know what you mean, oh Master Jackson?"

There is silence.

"Well?" I push.

Jackson ignores me. Quite. We push each other's buttons so well. He turns the volume up to the music, and we rock out to some old school Oasis.

Shelley

The navigation system said we had arrived at our destination, but we were on a dirt track in the middle of the forest.

"There!" Spotted Graham, "Turn right and continue for two miles for Lochfield Lodge."

Those two miles went fast, possibly due to the smoothing of the road with tarmac, something the website had mentioned, probably to entice city dwellers to journey up for short breaks. However, the road itself was framed with tall, dense woodland, and as we approached the lodge, we realised that it served as an elongated driveway.

I couldn't contain my excitement any longer; before Graham had even stopped the car, I jumped out and stepped onto the sprinkling of snow that glistened in the sun's light, giving the lodge an ethereal visage that made my heart flutter with eagerness to welcome my family.

"Quickly! There are lots of jobs to do before they get here." I reminded Graham before letting the now alert and officious Rubeus out of the car, so he could dubiously inspect the grounds in search of somewhere suitable for his afternoon constitutional.

I left Graham to unload the car and took a walk up the path from the car, which led to the spacious wooden porch - rather than cut across the snow peppered grass, of course. The porch had a lovely seating area on one side and patio doors on the other side. Next to the door, in the centre of the porch, there is a large ceramic plant pot with a rather forlorn plant inside, below which are the keys. I tilt the pot up and uncover just one key. I was sure the email said there would be two. I try the key in the door, and it opens. I double check the email, and it does say two keys 'for guests to enjoy freedom with their visit'. I find the number to phone if any issues arise; however, I still have no signal.

"Am I getting any help, Shell?" Graham called from the car.

I turn to give him a wink, but I am struck dumb at the vast landscape surrounding this perfect, isolated lodge. The view is split in two. One half is the narrow driveway sandwiched between two thick lengths of rich and green woods, and the other half is a vast and still loch surrounded by overlapping hills which reach beyond the horizon. And as I walk to the edge of the porch, I notice that the latter vista curves around the lodge's location and engulfs the entire backdrop of our weekend.

"Ahem!"

I turn around in fright as Graham is stood, laden down with bags and cases in a flustered but cheerful manner. I apologise and rush down to the car to help bring things in. Luckily, we brought food and drink for the weekend with us as the last shop we passed was more than forty miles down the road. I'd packed board games, snacks, spirits, mixers, and everything we'd need, including a vineyard's worth of wine.

Once the car was empty, we gave ourselves a tour of the lodge. This really is an impressively large lodge. As we walked in; immediately to the left, there was a bedroom, which would explain the patio doors onto the porch, and across from the front door, there was a staircase which led to 2 bedrooms and a lounge area supervising the loch with floor to ceiling windows covering a whole side of the lodge. Behind the stairs, another set leads down to another bedroom and a unique games room. The ground floor to the right was open plan and L-shaped with a plush kitchen, dining and lounge area, and just off the kitchen, there was a pantry with washing facilities and a large storage cupboard. This is perfect. Once satisfied with his sniffing tour of the lodge, Rubeus settled on the bed in one of the upstairs rooms and chewed on a stick he'd found on the grounds.

"Get off the bed with that thing!" Graham said, nudging the dog off the bed.

"Leave him be. He's happy." I retorted, giving my little fella a tummy tickle.

"I wonder how you'd react if I were to play with a dirty stick on the bed."

"Just you keep wondering!"

I smile to myself as I walk down the stairs, and I hear the sound of car doors slamming. I rush to the door to see who it is. Claire! It's Claire. My beautiful, strong girl. She seems unimpressed at my excitement. It's okay, I think to myself; I understand. Claire is my beautiful firstborn, and she's been through the mill this year. Until three months ago, she was level-headed and logical and focussed and had so much love to give. I cloak myself around her and kiss her cheek. Rubeus rushes out of the front door and straight to Mike: he's always liked Mike. We discuss the details of their drive while Graham helps Mike with their bags, and we head into the lodge.

"We thought you both might be comfortable upstairs next to us. It's a beautiful room, and the view is extraordinary." I offer to Claire and look to Mike for assurance.

"That sounds lovely. Thank you, Shelly." Mike nods toward me. He's terrific and so gentle.

I send them upstairs to get themselves sorted while Graham and I fix ourselves a drink. We play our song in the dining area and dance to Love Me Tender while we wait. Love Me Tender was our first dance at our wedding thirty five years ago, and we call it our charger. Whenever we are tired or sad or even just happy and content, we put it on and dance. It reminds us that everything is going to be okay; there is always a bigger picture to consider.

Before the song ends, the front door is swung open and in comes Kyle and Steven. My boys.

"Boys! Come in, come in." Graham ushers them in and takes their bags as I wrap myself around them both.

Kyle is my little smiler. He has been smiling since the day he was born and has always been the life and soul of the family, and Steven, Steven is the perfect addition to our family.

I notice they have only brought one bag with them and laugh to myself because men just don't need as much luggage as women. They, however, spy on me, judging their luggage.

"Some of us don't need to work hard to be beautiful!" Kyle jokes.

"And some of us are modest," Steven replies almost instantly.

Before I could even offer a tour, Kyle was away, bounding through the lower and ground floor of the lodge.

"Clairey fairy!" he bellowed, realising she must be upstairs and preparing himself to strike.

"Kyle!" I whispered as loud as I could, and in a slight panic, to prevent him from upsetting Claire, I tugged on his jumper as he tried to leap up the stairs. Then with a thud and a scream, his face smashed into the third stair. Before I could comprehend what was happening, my baby boy's smile was bloody, and Graham had readied a cloth filled with ice; Claire was laughing at the top of the stairs.

The next hour passed while we waited for Ellie and Jackson in an apologetic haze. Finally, we settled in the upstairs lounge with some wine: and an icepack. Claire would often let out a heart-warming giggle at Kyle's face, which would, in turn, lead to the whole room laughing. My family laughing together slightly overwhelmed me, and as I was overcome with emotion, I found myself crying. The last thing I want is the kids to be suspicious, so I rush away and into my bedroom. Graham follows me in with a worried look on his face.

"Did they notice?" I ask, still fighting back the tears.

"No. Just me." He takes me in his arms, and we dance to the muffled sound of conversation from next door. "I love you."

When we feel sufficiently recharged, I dab my eyes, and we head back through to the lounge area just in time to see that a car is leading up the drive and parking up behind Kyle and Steven's. It's Ellie and Jackson! We wave from the windows and head downstairs to welcome them in.

Ellie, my baby girl, is still yet to find her feet in the world. Luckily she's found Jackson, who keeps her feet on the ground. She was always my dreamer, longing to travel the world and make a difference in everyone's life.

I open the door, and Ellie squeezes me tight. "Love you, Mumma." She whispers in my ear before moaning about the lack of mobile phone reception and the lodge's location. Jackson bends down to kiss me on the cheek and to get through the door. He's so tall. Or I'm small.

The lodge is buzzing, and the atmosphere fills my heart with joy. I look out of the ground floor lounge window at the neat and untouched frosty snow across the grass, behind which the cars are tidily parked along the narrow road, and the loch is still and calming. Kyle takes Ellie and Jackson downstairs to their bedroom while Steven, Mike and Graham enjoy opening a bottle of whiskey in the dining area. Claire moves closer, wrapping her arm around me; she kisses me on the head and then leaves to go upstairs.

Just before dinner is ready, Ellie is setting the table and Graham and Mike have taken Rubeus out for a walk in the woods, so I decide to pop up the stairs to give myself a freshen up. As I wash my face in the dramatic sink, I look up and through into the bedroom from the mirror, and I swear I just saw one of the wardrobe doors move. It was as though it had bounced open, and I saw it shut. I walk out onto the landing and can hear everyone downstairs. What was it? There are no windows open to cause the wind to move it; in fact, it is considerably sturdy looking and wouldn't budge with wind anyway. I open the wardrobe door, and it is entirely empty. Strange. I guess I'm seeing things now.

Once I've almost finished changing, I can hear Rubeus bounding up the stairs to find me. He always likes to tell me all about his walks and show me any sticks he finds. My little fella. He comes in with fevered excitement and stops dead in his tracks between the door and me. Hesitantly, he sniffs around the bed and follows whatever scent he has picked up along the wall and right up to the wardrobe doors. I feel a chill up my spine as Rubeus begins to bark at the wardrobe, which I had seen seemingly close itself mere minutes ago. I approach the door as I am encouraged to do so by Rubeus's aggressive barking. I begin to shake as I find myself leaning in to open the door again. In a shot of adrenaline, I flap the door open, and for a split second, Rubeus is silent before growling warningly at the empty wardrobe. I stand staring into the bare cupboard, scared to move. Why was I scared? It is empty.

"Shell?" Graham calls from the bedroom door.

I swing around with a yelp. I scared myself. Or Rubeus had frightened me. "Everything alright?" When I didn't answer, Graham pried, and Rubeus had yet to avert his gaze from the empty wardrobe.

"Yes. Yes, sorry. Rubeus just seems to think the wardrobe is trying to attack us!"

"Oh my. Better watch out for those dangerous clothes! Dinner smells great, by the way." Graham says as he throws his hat and coat on the bed and chuckles his way down the stairs.

"It's empty, you fool!" I say discouragingly to Rubeus before closing the door and heading out of the bedroom. "Come on, little fella." Rubeus will not budge. I begin to get impatient and slightly agitated at his unwillingness to leave. "RUBEUS!" Luckily, Graham calls on him from down the stairs with a rattle of his dog food which flips a switch in his little head and makes him ping down like a whippet.

I stand in the doorway, staring at the wardrobe door. I turn the light off. I stare at the wardrobe door.

"MUM! Dinner!" Kyle shouts up.

"Coming! I'm coming." I close the door and roll my eyes as I walk down the stairs. That dog has spooked me.

Claire

In an attempt to fathom where we might be, I leant, ever so slightly, over the centre of the car to squint at the navigation system that had been positioned to point towards Mike. However, in a moment of muscle memory, Mike kissed my head. I shuddered in disgust and jolted back into my seat.

"What!?" He asked, slightly panicked.

"Nothing, nothing." I tried to say calmly while fighting off the urge to wretch.

"I thought you were…." Mike trailed off before finishing his sentence, sounding extremely disappointed.

Inside I wanted to make him happy. I wanted him never to sound sad or disappointed, but each time I'd go to say something nice to him, my body prevented me from speaking. I loved him. My husband is intelligent, resourceful, cheerful, optimistic, driven, ignorant, oblivious and flippant. No one is perfect, and I understand that. But, there is still just that swirling anger inside me, and I blame him for it. We had everything. We were going to be the perfect family. But, NO. Every time I think about what happened, I feel like my insides are trying to claw their way out of me. I'm not ready.

"We are here. Apparently." Mike suggested ending the awkward silence I'd caused.

"I got confused when you turned up onto the dirt track." I wanted to say in an upbeat tone, but it instead came out monotonously.

"There's a turn off ahead I'll use to do a doughnut and turn around." Mike jokingly said while looking at me for something. Anything that wasn't vacant. He didn't get what he wanted.

I saw a sign next to the turn off for Lochfield Lodge and presumed Mike had seen it too as he continued along the road without executing his aforementioned doughnut. It said two miles, but it felt like ten, being chased by giant trees which were trying to hide all evidence of daylight.

The road was smooth but thin; I couldn't imagine traffic being able to pass here: we'd be reversing all the way back if something came towards us. Up ahead, I can see mum and dad's car, and Mike pulls up just behind it, parking so close the proximity alarm is screaming at him to stop.

I step out of the car onto the frosted tarmac and breathe in the brisk air. There are hills and water and trees as far as I can see. Yet, there is no sign of life - just serenity.

"Claire!" I turn, and my mum is in my face, and before I can open my mouth to say hello, she is wrapped around my neck like a scarf. Or a noose. When she lets go, I can see her mouth moving, but she's speaking so fast in such an excitable tone I can barely catch a word. Dad pecks me on the cheek and goes to help Mike with our bags. Mum is pulling me towards the lodge, still talking. I catch a little about Rubeus, a little about Ellie and a little about wine. Wine sounds good. This really is a breathtakingly beautiful location. However, the lodge inside is contrastingly neutral and modern with cream sofas, white furniture, and large windows, which is a captivating juxtaposition to the outside. I suddenly realise there is silence and mum is staring at me. Did she just ask me a question? I wasn't listening. Oh lord, someone, please speak. I look at Mike, who thankfully seems to know what was asked.

"That sounds lovely; thank you, Shelly." Mike nods toward mum. He's always been the perfect addition to the family, fitting in from our first date when dad awkwardly interrogated him as he picked me up.

Mum starts to push us both towards the stairs, and I follow Mike, and a fervent Rubeus, up. When we reach the landing, I am stunned by the overwhelming view. There are floor to ceiling windows that cover the expanse of the upper floor, and oversized plush sofas fill the central space overlooking the Loch and surrounding hillside. To the left is mum's room: made evident by the impressive dog bed next to a bedside table where Rubeus is standing as if to show it off to us. Finally, we journey across the landing and into our room, which is also striking in size.

Mike begins unpacking the bags while I look around the room. The en-suite is also significant, with a roll top bathtub in the centre on a raised platform. My slippers have been placed tidily on the edge of the bed, and as I sit down to put them on, I can hear Love Me Tender being played from downstairs. Again, a wave of warmth and penitence washes over me. My mum and dad are my heroes. They've experienced pain, loss, and struggles, and they are still each other's best friends. I remember when I was really young, Kyle was just a baby, and dad had been in a car accident. He was in a coma for a few weeks and couldn't work or do much at all for months, and during that time, mum was nothing but a beacon of strength. She'd take us to the nursery, go to work, pick us up from nursery, give us dinner, drive to the hospital to see dad, then drive back with us sleeping in the back, put us to bed herself, and this went on for months. She was a single parent for almost a year, and it was not until three months ago, when Mike and I lost our baby, that mum and dad told us they had also lost a baby during that time. Mum had been seven months pregnant when dad had his accident, and the stress of the situation had caused her to go into early labour, and baby Austin was stillborn. So, of course, it helped to know what mum and dad had gone through when we had to lay our little girl to rest, but I can't imagine how she mourned during all that time without passing anything other than sanity to us - at the time.

I turn around to look at Mike and give him a look of remorse. Since the day we experienced our loss, I have been the worst wife, the worst friend, and the worst person. I didn't know how to deal with what was happening, and I couldn't accept Mike's method of mourning because he was positive. So positive, too positive. Probably for my benefit, and I'm the worst for not seeing how good he is. He smiles at me. A soft, gentle smile. How can being in this place for five minutes make me feel better? I think I feel positive, and I haven't felt positive in three months. I get up and walk to Mike, which I can tell makes him slightly panicked at my abnormal behaviour. When I reach him, I just place my head on his chest, and I can feel his heart racing as he precariously wraps his arms around me; as he does so, he slowly relaxes into our embrace, and we just stand there holding each other.

We stand there breathing with each other until there is a sudden scream from downstairs, and as Mike and I rush out to see if everything is ok, I see Kyle looking up at me with his face covered in blood and mum holding on to his top. He looks at mum, who begins to apologise profusely before looking at me incredulously through the blood. Finally, I couldn't hold it anymore, and I burst into laughter. I don't know precisely what has happened, but it's perfect; the attention won't be on me while Kyle has a bloody face! We rush down to help, but quick thinking, dad, is there in seconds with a wet cloth and an ice pack. I kiss Steven hello and laugh in Kyle's face. Once he's cleaned up, we all go upstairs with a few bottles of wine to recover from what just happened and to wait on Ellie and Jackson.

Upstairs we discuss Steven's new promotion, and I can't help but laugh every time I look at Kyle; of all the people to have a fat lip, he would definitely take it the worst. I notice mum seems a bit emotional, but she always is on these weekends. A few years ago, when we went to the Lake District, she spent more time blubbing away than not, continually saying how thankful she was for us. I'm happy she's happy, though. Wait. Am I happy? I'm happy! I look at Mike and smile. I just smiled at Mike! Oh, bless him, that's the first time I've smiled at him in three months. He deserved that. I can't believe that this; being with my family on holiday is helping.

It's two bottles of wine later when the final two arrive, which is exciting because Ellie always brings with her a majestic atmosphere, and Jackson gets on so well with Steven and Mike. We welcome them downstairs, and she's just as effervescent and grousing as ever. The family is complete. Everyone goes their separate ways, noting we'll be back together at five for dinner, so we have an hour to get ourselves sorted. I leave to go upstairs but notice mum is standing staring out of the window in the lounge area. She's perfect: the epitome of class. I go to her and hold her for a moment. I don't say anything; I just hope she can feel how much she means to me. I kiss her on the head and go upstairs for a shower.

I feel dirty and want to wash off the mist of negativity I've carried with me for so long. I consider having a bath in the rather dramatic bath scene, but I can't resist the multi-head rainfall massage shower. Mum has done really well with accommodation this year. I throw off my clothes and realise that I am being presented to the Scottish Highlands via the sheet of glass between us and run to the bathroom. There are two entrances to the bathroom: one at either side of the wardrobe on the left-hand side of the bedroom. I get into the shower and turn up the heat. I've always loved a hot shower.

Mike comes in while I'm in the shower, and I feel a slight flutter in my heart. The flutter could be the wine. Or the flutter could be that he hasn't seen me naked in over three months. He obviously knew I was in the shower because he would have heard the water running. Does he want to see me naked, or does he just need the toilet? I can't see anything through the glass because of the steam. Say something.

"The shower is amazing. We should definitely think about getting something like this in the house." I say, surprising myself with my light tone, and I can see him now standing about a metre away.

"You're going to love it when you get in." I try to say in a suggestive tone, but I'm being too conversational, although he moves a little closer.

"It's a really great temperature. Nice and hot." Seriously? "Just the way I like it." Stop! Three months with no sex, and I now sound like an inexperienced stripper.

He moves back. I try and look sexy through the steam as I lather the shampoo in my hair.

"Did you want to come in...now?" Oh lord, I sound pathetic.

"With me..." What am I saying? I feel like a teenager saying all the wrong things.

I start to laugh. I'm speaking to my husband at the end of the day.

"Say something, Mike. I'm making a fool of myself here. I think it's the wine from earlier!"

Mike doesn't say anything, and I can't see him anymore. I pop my head out of the shower door.

"Mike?" I ask the room.

Nothing. He must have left. Maybe I was too much. He's been dealing with irrational and cold Claire for so long that maybe I've scared him off with the old Claire. To be fair, I'm scaring myself with the old Claire being back with a vengeance. It's like a switch has flipped in my head. I can't believe within mere hours how much my mindset has altered. What if Mike wants to leave me? It was a mutual decision to give ourselves the ultimatum. Maybe he has already decided. I finish in the shower and get ready with all these thoughts flying around, and once I'm ready, I run down to find Mike, but he's out walking the dog with dad.

I sit in the lounge area with Ellie for a while, waiting on Mike to come back, jumping between decisions of what to do in my head. The door opens. Rubeus runs in, and bolts upstairs as dad follows with a nod to us before heading upstairs too. And Mike comes in, closes the door, turns around, and I kiss him. I tell him I love him. He thinks for a moment. He picks me up and returns my kiss. We look at each other. He tells me he loves me. We stare at each other.

"If you're hungry for something that isn't a stealthy staring contest, dinner is ready." Kyle interrupted us.

"Thanks." I muster, barely able to detract my gaze from Mike.

"I'm sorry." I say to Mike as we make our way to the dining area.

"Never be sorry. I love you." He whispers as he squeezes my hand.

"MUM! Dinner!" Kyle shouts up the stairs.

Kyle

"Jeez. If remote was what your mum wanted, she's got it. And some."

The navigation system wants me to turn up this dirt track, but that can't be right, surely? "Have you seen any sign of life?" I ask Steven in the hope of not being lost.

"Not for at least half an hour. The website did say it was up a 'country road' though and that it would smooth out for us halfway up."

Thank goodness. I exhale with a sound of relief and take the turn as advised. I can see the temperature dropping on the car's thermometer. I never packed any jackets or jumpers, so I hope mum has the heating on when we get there.

"So we will suss the atmosphere tonight and tomorrow, and if, if, we feel that everyone is in an open and appreciative mood, we will tell everyone on Sunday. Agreed?"

"Agreed," Steven confirms militantly. "I feel like we are on a film set. This is such a beautiful and underrated part of the country."

"Trees. Hills. Apparently, there's a loch nearby. It's not exactly a rarity." I sarcastically respond.

As I drive further up this road, I feel like I'm in one of those never-ending optical illusions, and just as I'm getting dizzy, I spot the lodge. The door is just closing. Rude. I park immediately behind Claire and Mike's hideous estate car, and we get out and stretch our legs.

"There's your apparent loch." Steven points to the loch and comes over and kisses me. I grab the bag from the back of the car, and we walk up to the porch. We walk on the path which leads round to the porch, pop our bag down next to the door and soak in the view.

"It's freezing, but it's beautiful." I say, nuzzling into Steven's chest while looking over the porch.

"Breath-taking," Steven says in a speechless tone. "I love you." He adds, squeezing me tighter.

The window next to the door is open, and I hear Love Me Tender start to play in the lodge and the biggest smile forms on my face. My mum and dad are my relationship inspiration. They have played Love Me Tender and danced to it together nearly every day for over thirty years. They call it their charger, as though it regenerates their energy levels. They are perfect! Romantically, Steven starts to dance with me on the porch, but he's leading, so it ends swiftly in a fumble and a chuckle. I kiss him, go and pick up the bag and open the door.

Dad instantly rushes over, hugs us and takes the bag from me. Mum is a bit slower to come over, and I notice she looks a little tired. I give her a big smile and hug. We get shown our room which is just to the left of the front door. We have patio doors which lead out onto the porch to the exact spot Steven and I had just been, and it is host to a beautiful view over the loch filled glen. It's a cosy room with light wooden furniture, neutral linens and tartan flares. There's a mirror the width of the bed above the headboard, which gives the illusion that the room is much larger. The en-suite to the back of the room is almost as big as the room itself, with a two-way walk-in shower and a his-and-his sink. There's a small cupboard immediately on the left; I open it, and an icy draft escapes, so I close it instantaneously.

I come back through to the bedroom and notice mum eyeing up our singular bag. "Some of us don't need to work hard to be beautiful!" I offer cheekily with a wink. "And some of us are modest." Steven replies almost instantly. I already knew I hadn't packed enough, but we'd packed in a rush, and it wasn't like we were going out anywhere. We were spending the whole weekend in one place with the family - no one to impress here.

I get bored, waiting to be offered a tour, so I give myself one while Steven talks to mum and dad about the drive. As I turn around the staircase, I notice there is another staircase leading down. A basement? Fun. I go down, and there are three doors. One door is locked. I presume it must be the owner's belongings or a cleaning cupboard or something. One door leads to a massive bedroom; a four-poster bed looks lost in the oversized room and loads of antique furniture: a far cry from the contemporary feeling upstairs. The third door opens to a games room where there is a bar in the corner, a dart board, a pool table and a television on the wall. There is another door in the games room that also appears to be locked. Annoying. I'm nosey.

I run upstairs to explore more. The ground floor is all open plan, aside from our room, with stylish and minimal décor throughout. The dining area is luscious with cream, high-backed dining chairs around a thick wooden dining table. The kitchen is enormous with an island and worktops of marble. There is a small room just off the kitchen with shelving and washing facilities and a tiny, almost pointless, cupboard that is so small; all it houses is a mop and a brush.

I still haven't found Claire. She must be upstairs. I run around and spring to attack the stairs three at a time. "Clairey Fairy!" I shout as I take my first leap. In a dream of confusion, I think I'm flying for a split second and, again in confusion, feel weightless. Even before I had a chance to acknowledge my confusion, my head had smashed down onto a stair, and my face began to feel cold. I lay dumbfounded for a few moments. What on Earth happened? I get up and look to the top of the stairs and see Claire in a fit of laughter, Mike behind her contrastingly shocked. I turn around and see mum is holding my top. Why is she holding my top? Dad arrives with a wet cloth and an ice pack. Steven takes the cloth from dad and starts to paw at my face. I feel freezing cold. I think I'm just in shock. Claire and Steven begin to lead me upstairs.

"What...happened?" I ask in a shiver.

"I'm so sorry, baby." Mum said before shedding a tear. "I just didn't want you upsetting Claire."

"Oh, mum! You're hilarious." Claire rebutted.

I couldn't believe my mum. I was, however, surprised at how well I was dealing with the situation. Because Claire kept laughing at me, and we hadn't heard Claire laugh for months, I didn't mind too much being the butt of the joke.

We all went upstairs, and mum ploughed us with wine. Quite right. We chatted about Steven's new promotion, and everyone was really relaxed. I had almost forgotten about the growing lump on my face, and if it hadn't been for the throbbing reminder whenever I made any form of facial expression, I would definitely have elapsed the ordeal. Wine, nevertheless, was working wonderfully as a painkiller. I notice mum getting emotional while we are all laughing. Bless her. She really loves us.

While we are sitting in the upstairs lounge looking out on the calming view, we spy Ellie and Jackson driving up the narrow road in their rather dilapidated looking car. They park up directly behind our car. The only way I can see us leaving on Monday is by reversing, in convoy, the whole way down the road.

I love Ellie. She's my mischievous little sister who is always up for causing a little raucous. Claire and I were the competitive over-achievers and were extremely orderly children - and adults. However, due to complacency after the successful behaviours of Claire and me, mum's lax discipline when it came to Ellie led to her facilitation of a wayward lifestyle as a teenager. She has, in recent years, found Jackson, who has helped her keep her feet on the ground: and out of trouble.

"What the hell happened to your face? You look awful. Well, not too much more awful than normal." Ellie jibed as we walked down the stairs. I stopped and shoved her bag into her hands.

"Carry your bag yourself to your dungeon!" I said as I sassily slunk down the remainder of the stairs. "Mum decided I was too beautiful and destroyed my face in a momentary lapse of sanity." I added to an applause of laughter from both Jackson and Ellie.

"You're just as nuts as she is." Jackson said while containing his laughter.

"It's true, though! I went running up the stairs, and she literally pulled me down."

"OK, Kyle!" Ellie said, pushing her way past me into her room.

I could tell she was a bit angry to be downstairs. There was very little light down here because the windows were small and only at the top of the walls. It also felt a lot less inviting than the rest of the lodge, and I don't know whether he was fed up with Ellie's company, whether he could sense her frustration or whether he genuinely felt irritable, but Jackson immediately changed and went for a run. He has the body of Adonis, so I didn't mind him changing at all. Once he left, we sat on the sofa in the corner of the room.

"Spill the beans, jellybean. How are you both?" I ask anxiously, feeling like Ellie wanted to get something off her chest.

"We're good." She said hesitantly.

"You sure?" I pried not sounding too invested.

We stare at each other in silence for a bit. Usually, I would push her to talk to me, and we could work out any issues she might have, but this time I really don't want to. This time I can't bring myself to care about the trivialities of her relationship issues. I think she might just need to grow up and get over herself this time.

"I'm sure." Finally, she gives in and slumps down on the sofa pulling me in for a hug.

Thank goodness. I do love her, but sometimes she can be a bit of a drama queen. We are slumped in a cuddle, and it feels like the house is empty. There is silence down here. I kiss Ellie on the head, get up and pull my pretzel of a sister up to her feet. I show her to the games room, and we play a round of darts. I've never been very good at darts or any sport, really. Ellie, on the other hand, is a pretty good shot.

"What was that?" Ellie asked quizzically.

"What?"

"That noise." She replied, putting the darts down and going to the hall. She checked the bedroom, but Jackson still wasn't back, and no one was there. I never heard anything, but she seemed rather adamant. She tried to open the door that was locked with no success. "What's in there?"

"Pass. It was locked when we arrived."

She pressed her ear to the door and then beckoned me to join her. A light, airy sound was through the door that moved like a wave. "It sounds like it's the boiler room or something," I said dismissively. "What did you hear initially?"

"It was like a door closing." Ellie said, not content with my explanation.

She disappeared into her room and reappeared with a little tool kit. I watched an expert at work as she toyed her way around the keyhole with multiple metal implements until there was a precise and heavy sounding click. She looked at me with a smile that covered her whole face.

"I don't want to know why, or where, or when you learned how to do that." I said before helping her back to her feet.

"Ladies first." She said, pointing to the door and looking at me.

"Sexist criminal." I rolled my eyes and turned the door handle. The door opened ever so slightly. It was just enough for the latch to come unhooked, but it wouldn't open any further. It wouldn't even open enough for there to just be a crack in the door frame. I tried to push it open, but it wouldn't budge; it was as though there was a solid and tight chain latched on the inside. I didn't want to push too hard in case I damaged the door, but wrecking ball Ellie still wasn't happy. She again disappeared and returned with another felonious apparatus.

"This should get us in." She said, sliding the thin piece of metal down the slither that the door had opened. She got all the way down and looked puzzled. "Nothing is holding the door shut."

"There must be something in the way. The owners probably put whatever it is there, so pests like you don't get in!"

"Shhhh." Ellie silenced me with a flick of her hand while her head remained pressed against the open end of the door.

I joined her, and I heard the same thing again. A light, airy sound that moved like a wave. Almost like someone breathing. That was it. Like someone breathing. In. And out. I look at Ellie, and her eyes are locked on mine.

"What are you two up to?" Steven interrupts, coming down the stairs and frightening us both.

"Nothing. Kyle is just causing trouble." Ellie jokingly responds, pulling the door closed and visibly shaking herself off.

"How dare you!" I respond incredulously.

"Your mum wants help with dinner. Claire is resting; Jackson is out being fit, Mike and your dad are walking Rubeus, and I'm setting up the games, so you two are required." Steven debriefs as he pulls us both up the stairs.

Ellie

I cannot fathom why mum would want to be so far
isolated from reality. This drive has been never-ending.
Every time Jackson has flicked his indicator, I've thought
that surely we must be there now, but no. Every time he
inhaled deeply, I'd think he would announce our
imminent arrival, but no. Every time I looked at the
navigation system, I'd pray it would have dropped
drastically in miles-left-to-go since the last time I looked
at it, but no. Every time a good song would come on and
distract me, I'd think this is the song that will help me
forget how bored I am, but no.

"Are you taking the piss and driving in circles?" I ask
impatiently.

"Yes. I'd just waste all of that petrol and time just to
annoy you." Jackson replied rather crabbily.

"Don't snap at me!" I huff. "I didn't realise there were
so many fields in Scotland. We must have passed the

world's supply of potato." I offer jokingly as my way of apology for being impetuous.

"Most of these fields will be used for grazing out with the winter months. Probably no potatoes."

Here we go again; sometimes, I feel very dumb with Jackson. There's always an opportunity to correct me or prove me wrong. We turn up a dirt track that the navigation system seems confident with, and Jackson appears sure to trust.

The car is struggling along this road, and the navigation system tells us we've arrived.

"I knew this was a wrong turn. You can't always trust satnavs." I burst. I couldn't hold it in any longer.

"You've wanted to say that since we turned off, haven't you?"

"Yes." I affirm.

Jackson keeps driving, and just up ahead, there's a small signpost pointing to another dirt track turn off for Lochfield Lodge. At the sign, just before the turn-off,

Jackson slows down the car and turns to look at me with a snide, smug smile.

"You're lucky I am more annoyed at the fact that there are another two miles on a dirt track than I am with your arrogance right now."

Jackson is still chuckling to himself when we pull up behind Kyle's car, and we see everyone waving from the most enormous window I've ever seen in my life. That's an impressive looking lodge. I was expecting an oversized garden shed.

We grab our bags from the car and head up the path to the lodge. Mum swings the door open and welcomes me in with a hug. I squeeze her tight. Gosh, I love her. "I love you, Mumma." I whisper in her ear before giving everyone else hugs.

"Can you believe there's no mobile signal for at least fifty miles?" I say incredulously to Kyle. "I love you all, but this is more remote than I've been in some third world countries!" Everyone laughs. I forgot my family think I'm funny. "Oh, it's lovely, don't get me wrong." I say sarcastically. "I just feel like I'm in flipping quarantine!"

Inside, the lodge was beautiful. Pretty impressive, really. There were lots of cupboards everywhere, which are always handy. Wait a minute. There are no curtains. Anywhere. What's that all about?

"There's no curtains." I point out to Jackson. "Anywhere." I reiterate, looking around the house.

"I suppose we are so secluded out here there's no need for them." He offers wisely.

True, I guess. Kyle takes my bag and leads us to the hidden staircase around the corner.

"What the hell happened to your face? You look awful. Well, not too much more awful than normal." I pushed Kyle's buttons as we walked down the stairs. I should have thought it through; however, as he stopped and shoved my bag into me.

"Carry your bag yourself to your dungeon!" He said while flouncing down the stairs. "Mum decided I was too beautiful and destroyed my face in a momentary lapse of sanity." he added to an applause of laughter from both Jackson and me.

"You're just as nuts as she is." Jackson said while containing his laughter.

"It's true, though! I went running up the stairs, and she literally pulled me down." Kyle was almost pleading for us to believe him. I did. I just like winding him up.

"OK, Kyle!" I said, pushing my way past him jokingly into our bedroom.

I was furious to be in the basement bedroom. No light. No warmth. No life. It's a massive room as well; such a poor space utilisation. At least we have an en-suite.

On the other hand, it's a bit small. It appears that the whole lodge is beautifully modern and stylish: except for our cellar. It makes sense, though. Claire is definitely the favourite, at the top of the house, Kyle is the second favourite in the middle, and I'm forgotten about and sent to the basement. It's comical, really.

Jackson seems agitated and decides to go for a run as soon as we've put the bags on the bed. I can tell he's frustrated after the long drive. I feel restless, and I'm five foot three inches. He's six foot four, so he must be antsy. He gets changed in front of Kyle, and I and I can see Kyle staring. Jackson's body is pretty perfect, and he likes to wear tight underwear, so I don't mind. Plus, Steven is just as dishy. Kyle is just as lucky. Well. Maybe not just as lucky.

Jackson leaves, and Kyle and I take a seat on an old antiquated sofa. I want Kyle to ask if everything is OK. I need Kyle to ask me what's wrong.

"Spill the beans, jellybean. How are you both?" Kyle asks, right on cue. He calls me jellybean because when I was a toddler, I snuck into his room and stole his jellybeans, but; as karma would have it, I ended up choking, and if it hadn't been for Kyle finding me and slapping me on the back, I might have choked to death. Plus, it is not dissimilar to Ellie, I suppose.

"We're good." I say, trying to make Kyle probe further.

"You sure?" Kyle continued like a puppet on a string.

We stare at each other in silence for a bit. Normally Kyle would push me to talk about what was upsetting me, but he wasn't this time. This time I really needed him to. This time the issue isn't trivial and immature. This time the problem isn't about me at all. This time I need to talk to my big brother. This time I don't know what to do. This time I need help. Kyle?

"I'm sure." Finally, I give up and pull him in for a hug.

Why would he not push me to speak? I moan to Kyle all the time about family, work, Jackson, and life in general. He's probably sick fed up with me. I've probably ruined my chances of ever receiving advice again because of my stupid immaturity. I don't know how much longer I can keep this a secret. I don't know what to do. I curl up and bury my head in Kyle's chest.

Kyle picks me up and drags me across the hall. It's a games room, which is pretty cool. Inside is a pool table and a darts board; I am pretty awesome at winning those two games. Excellent. There's also a bar, a huge TV and a locked cupboard. Another cupboard. So many cupboards. I spy the darts sitting on the bar and hit a bull's eye before Kyle turns to look at me. He picks up the other set and feebly challenges me to a match.

I was winning by a country mile and was just about to throw a dart when I heard a door click shut. I wondered if Jackson had come home. He'd have heard us and said hi, surely?

"What was that?" I asked Kyle, thinking he'd confirm it to be Jackson.

"What?" He replied innocently.

"That noise." I said, putting the darts down and going to the hall. The bedroom door was open, and I could see that no one was in there; the en-suite was empty too. I definitely heard a door click shut. There was a door in-between my bedroom and the games room. It had to be that one. Kyle never showed me in there on his tour. "What's in there?" I pointed to the closed door.

"Pass. It was locked when we arrived." Kyle shrugged, watching me in bafflement.

I tried to open it for my own sanity, and it was indeed locked. I pressed my ear to the door to see if I could hear anything. I could. There was a sound like a scuffle of feet on gravel, then silence. I waved Kyle to come over and listen too. While we concentrated, a light, airy sound came through the door that moved like a wave. "It sounds like it's the boiler room or something." Kyle said after a minute dismissively. "What did you hear initially?"

"It was like a door closing." I told him sharply.

I knew what I heard, and now I was even more certain it was this door. Kyle hadn't listened to the first two noises. I bet it will be Jackson or Steven playing a prank. I went and got my tool kit and took it to the door. As I was picking the lock, I could feel Kyle's dumbfounded stare on my hands, and I was about to say something when I found the bite, twisted with my thumb and index and unlocked the door with a precise and heavy sounding click. I looked at Kyle feeling appropriately conceited.

"I don't want to know why or where or when you learned how to do that." Kyle said disapprovingly while helping me up.

I could tell he was impressed. "Ladies first." I said, winking at Kyle and gesturing to the door.

"Sexist criminal." He rolled his eyes and turned the door handle. The door opened ever so slightly. It was just enough for the latch to come unhooked, but it wouldn't open any further. Damn. It wouldn't even open enough for there to just be a crack in the door frame. Kyle tried to push it open, but it wouldn't budge; I tried as well, and it was as though there was an extremely strong and tight chain latched on the inside. I wasn't happy because we've come this far. I will get into that room. I ran to get my metal ruler. I hid the measurement markings from Kyle, and he looked scared when I came out of the bedroom.

"This should get us in." I say, sliding the ruler down the slither that the door had opened. I was expecting the ruler to be stopped at some point by a latch or an object in the way, but it slid all the way down. "Nothing is holding the door shut." I told Kyle.

"There must be something in the way. The owners probably put whatever it is there, so pests like you don't get in!" He rebutted impatiently.

I rolled my eyes at him and put my ear to the open slither. "Shhhh." If he'd shut up, I could maybe hear more. This time I listened to the airy sound much clearer.

Kyle joined me in a bit of a strop. The light, airy sound that moved like a wave. Almost like someone breathing. That was it. Like someone breathing. In. And out. I look at Kyle and wait a few seconds until his eyes are locked on mine.

"What are you two up to?" Steven interrupts, coming down the stairs and frightening us both.

"Nothing. Kyle is just causing trouble." I jibe while pulling the door completely shut behind me. Kyle was probably right. It probably is the boiler room. For goodness sake. Not being able to use my phone is making me mad.

"How dare you!" Kyle responds with a flounce.

"Your mum wants help with dinner. Claire is resting; Jackson is out being fit, Mike and your dad are walking Rubeus, and I'm setting up the games, so you two are required." Steven debriefs as he pulls us both up the stairs.

All

I look around at my beautiful children all sitting around the dining table. I look at the beautiful partners they have chosen. They are laughing and conversing, and I feel like my heart can't get any fuller. I am filled with love. I am filled with gratitude. I am filled with content. I spy Graham topping up everyone's glasses. He has always been good at maintaining a steady flow of wine at dinners and tonight was no exception; each person appeared to be enjoying the delicious social lubricant. I've always liked wine. I think it's a sophisticated drink. I don't know why but I've always felt rather educated and cultured holding a glass of wine.

When the children were little, Graham and I gifted them a small wine glass with their names on it for each of their fifth birthdays. That way, when we enjoyed wine with dinner; or at a party, as did the kids. It was a small glass. Around a fifth of a large glass. I wasn't in the habit of inebriating my children. However, I believe, as a direct result of our Mediterranean parenting style, they never grew up abusing alcohol. They never grew up getting drunk at parties. They respected us as we respected them. They learnt to appreciate and respect alcohol as well since it was never taboo for them. But most importantly, they would never hide anything from us as we would never hide anything from them.

There have only ever been two things we have chosen to remain untold. The first was something we faced a little under thirty years ago when Graham had his accident.

Graham had been involved in a car accident that left him in a coma. I was beside myself with panic and fear, and I missed him dreadfully. Claire was just old enough to tie her shoelaces, and Kyle had only just begun stumbling through the house. The stress of the entire situation forced me into a very early labour, and our third little baby, Austin, was stillborn. The day I was in the hospital saying goodbye to Austin was also the day Graham came out of his coma. I was so thankful. Of course, we mourned our loss, but without Graham as my husband

and my best friend, I cannot fathom how I would have survived this life.

The second thing that we have decided to remain untold for the foreseeable future is just as frightening. I've lived a wonderfully exciting life. A rich life with a family and husband I am very proud of. But I'm not ready to go. Not yet. I'm not yet sixty. I need to see grandchildren first, at least.

"Right, everyone, retire upstairs, and your dad and I will do the dishes." I shoo everyone away from the table.

"There's a dishwasher, mum." Ellie says dryly.

"Your dad has a name, Ellie." I joke.

They go upstairs, taking more wine with them and Graham and I stare at each other in contentment while we load the dishwasher and clear the table. Rubeus follows our every move around our feet.

"Everything is going to be alright, you know." I tell Graham.

"Is it now?" He replies, sounding pleased with my display of positivity.

"Yes. I'm going to get better. I'm going to meet my grandchildren. We are going to go on a safari. We are going to bring up little Rubeus. We are only halfway through our lives, and I'm not leaving you to do all that alone."

My husband is a very gentle and caring man but in thirty-five years of marriage, I can count on one hand how many times he has shed a tear. So now, as his eyes glisten in the warm, dimmed light of the lodge, I am stricken with a surge of strength. I put the tea towel I have in my hand down, walk to my husband, put my head on his chest, and we sway. He takes my hand, and we dance.

-

As we are all heading upstairs to play some board games, I can see Jackson shutting down. Since he returned from his run, he has been in his own world and hasn't talked to me.

"Seriously, what's wrong, babe?" I held back on the stairs and walked up with him.

"Nothing." He monotonously responded.

"You're being pretty distant and not joining in. Have I done something?" I felt like I'd upset him somehow. This was not, however, uncommon for him.

"No. I'm just tired." He offered without looking at me.

Once we reached the top of the stairs, he stood there for a moment longer than I, transfixed, looking out of the towering windows. The sun had almost completely disappeared, and the evening dusk had settled in on the little loch-filled glen. The hills were barely visible, and there was only a light shimmer on the water, which I had to strain to see. Soon it would be pitch black, and only we would be visible to the Scottish nature like fish in a tank.

"Who's in the bag?" Claire drunkenly asked.

"Absolutely!" Kyle and Steven excitably replied in sync.

Who's in the bag is a family favourite game that we generally play in teams of two, and usually in our respective couples. One person gets a minute to pull out names of famous people from a bag, and they must describe that person without saying their name, while the other team player has to guess who it is. Each round lasts a minute, and the team with the most names at the end wins.

Tonight, however, we opted to play in teams of four: Mum and the partners and dad and the children. Claire was first up to describe for our team.

"She plays Bridget Jones."

"Bridget Jones!" Kyle screamed.

"Renee Zellweger." I corrected him through laughter.

"He comes at Christmas."

"Santa." I calmly answer.

"I KNOW HIM!" Kyle jokes.

"She's ancient."

"CHER!" Kyle shrieks.

"Kyle, we are all in the same room!" I say as I punch him on the arm.

"Wow, you're good at this!" Claire slurred, flabbergasted that Kyle guessed it so quickly. "You put it on your plants to make them grow."

"Fertiliser." Dad assumed.

"No. It's green."

"Green fertiliser." Dad reiterated.

"No. It's sometimes brown."

"Poo?" I hesitantly offered.

"NO! It's a person's name. She's a model." Claire agitatedly told us.

Everyone was crying with laughter, and Claire was getting cross.

"Miss Fertiliser." Dad offered, cracking himself up even more while he did so.

"TIME!" Steven shouted.

"Who was it?" Kyle enquired while wiping his tears away.

"Kate Moss." Claire said through gritted teeth.

"Moss? MOSS!" The entire room descended into delirious laughter, much to Claire's chagrin.

"Moss grows like a weed, Claire. You don't want to put it on things. It definitely won't make them grow!" Mike educated Claire patronisingly as he got up and kissed her.

I loved these moments with my family. We've always been really good at laughing at ourselves. If we fell over as kids, mum and dad would be the first to laugh at us, and that rubbed off on our outlooks on life. If something negative happened, we'd laugh it off and say things could be worse. If we found ourselves to be embarrassed, we'd laugh at each other. There's no point in being timid and worrying too much. Life's too short.

We are still trying to suppress the resurgence of laughter that has occurred to allow the other team to play their turn, but as one person giggles, like a domino effect, the entire room falls into a pool of hilarity. Through tears, I look round at Jackson, who is sat stony-faced and is apparently unmoved by the merriment. Whatever, I think. He can just be that guy who doesn't have fun. He turns to look at me and then gets up and disappears. He reappears a minute later and hands me a drink.

"Sorry, babe." He kisses me on the head and returns to his team. Oh. Maybe he is just tired. This drink is lovely.

-

The stairs were definitely moving under my feet. I felt like I was floating, and the stairs were sliding behind me. My feet seemed to dangle in the air as I tried to step on the ground. Wow. I wish Steven were here for this. I look round and see Steven just to my right.

"Steven!" I try and kiss him but can't move my body closer to him.

"I'm floating." I tell him in astonishment.

"You are floating, aren't you? You're so clever." He tells me, and I feel there's an air of disdain in his voice.

I hear laughter behind me, and I turn my head to see Mike. "Hi, Mike! What are you doing?"

"Trying to help, bud!" Mike said with a wink.

Don't wink at me. You're like my brother. Goodness me.

Oh no. I'm falling. Oh lord. Not again. Wait. That was a soft landing. What's happened? I spread my arms out and feel softness. Bed! I'm in bed. Wondrous.

"Are you going to get ready for bed, princess?" Steven asks me as I am still face down on the bed.

I turn round on the bed and look at my husband undressing. His perfect body is struggling to get a jumper off. I laugh, and he notices me watching him. He walks toward me, and I lift my legs and hint for him to undress me too. He slides my shoes and socks off and comes in towards me for a kiss. As he kisses me, he undoes the buttons on my shirt and pulls it off. I find my hands on his belt; I whip it open and pop all his jeans buttons at once.

"Someone has sobered up." Steven teases me as he removes the rest of his clothes, and I mine.

We make love and end in a cuddle on the sofa at the foot of the bed. My husband is amazing. I am the luckiest boy in the world. I look at Steven and find he's looking at me with a smile.

"Let's go to bed, Ste." I say as I tidy the bed covers and switch off the lamps. We lie in bed and look out the patio door windows. Someone has left the lounge light from upstairs on as it's shining out the front of the lodge, and I can make out the shapes of trees in the distance. I can't be bothered getting up to turn it off, though, so I just close my eyes.

I open my eyes and notice the light has gone from upstairs. Someone must have turned it off. I look out of the patio door windows into the darkness. It must be windy because I can only just make out the treetop outlines moving wildly. At that moment, I hear a noise coming from what sounds like the kitchen. I listen intently and realise it's just Ellie or Jackson as I listen to them descend the stairs to their bedroom. I need to pee. I walk, or stumble, to the bathroom. I'm definitely still a little drunk. As I turn on the light in the bathroom, I turn back into the bedroom to avoid blistering my corneas where I look through the patio door windows, and my eyes fall on a handprint. On the right-hand pane of glass and two thirds up, there is a greasy handprint made visible by the bathroom light shining through. That definitely wasn't there before. It must have been when we were having sex. I grab the hand towel from the bathroom and go to clean it off. It won't come off. I push harder, but it won't budge. Then it hits me; it's on the outside. That's weird. I'm sure I never noticed it there before. I unlock the door and swing it open to quickly rub off the dirty handprint. It comes off easily, and I shut it before going to the toilet and crawling back to bed.

-

I'm incredibly thankful and proud of myself for switching from wine to water a few hours ago as I watch Steven and Mike carry Kyle down the stairs. I tidy the lounge up a bit, and when Mike returns, we go to the bedroom. I think I'll leave the light on in the lounge - just in case anyone gets up in the night and loses their bearings.

"How are you?" Mike asks lovingly; since we have actually not had the opportunity to talk this evening. Not since I kissed him on his return from walking Rubeus.

"I am good. Really good, Mike." I respond with a smile while I slowly remove my jumper. I'm not going to make the shower mistake again. I look down at myself. Stood in my trousers and bra. I look at Mike, scared he might be repulsed. He doesn't say anything; he opens his mouth as though he is about to, but he appears to be speechless. Is that a good or a bad thing? I wish he'd say either way. Please, Mike. He looks me in the eye. He removes his jumper.

He stood at one side of the bed and I at the other, taking it in turns to remove our clothing. We stand naked, my stomach imperfect from what happened three months ago, and his stomach has grown ever so slightly outward. The lamps in the room emit a warm light that fills the room with a glow, and I begin to notice my senses heightening. There's a frill on the bed cover that is tickling my thigh. I can't believe I've not seen my husband naked for three months. I can see him becoming aroused while he is looking at me, and we both smirk like school kids. Mike makes the first move as he climbs onto the bed and pulls me up on the other side. He kisses me softly, and I kiss him harder. He presses his body against mine, and I feel a flurry of warmth and adrenaline shoot through my body. His body is perfect, and as I run my hands down his back and onto his bum, I begin to cry. Feeling embarrassed, I pull away from Mike to wipe my eyes, but he holds me still and wipes them for me. He has welled up too.

We make love.

It is beautiful.

"I love you so much." I say with my head on Mike's chest, listening to his heartbeat slow down as he regains his breath.

"You're perfect. You are my everything. I love you." He returns as he kisses my head and leaves to go and brush his teeth.

"I was so scared I'd ruined everything after earlier on today." I call through to Mike in the bathroom.

"What happened earlier on today?" Mike came through with a mouth full of foamed toothpaste.

"You know..." I say, raising my eyebrow at him, to which he responds with a blank expression.

"When I made a fool of myself in the shower." I embarrassingly reminded him.

"What did you do in the shower?" Mike asked curiously with a chuckle.

"Mike. When you came into the bathroom, and I was showering." I was annoyed he was making me relive it.

"I never came into the bathroom while you were showering, Claire." Mike seemed a bit more innocent and cautious now.

"You did. Just before you took Rubeus for a walk with dad."

"No, Claire, I never." Mike said firmly.

"Well, who did? I made an absolute fool of myself thinking it was you."

"It was probably Kyle or Steven."

"Yeah, and they wouldn't have said anything because I made an absolute tit of myself inviting who I thought was you to join me." I felt sick with embarrassment while Mike couldn't contain his laughter.

-

I jolt awake and hear Rubeus stretching. I look at the clock, and it's not yet three in the morning. I thought I heard a bang, but it was probably just my dream waking me up. I look at Graham, and he's still sound asleep. I smile to myself, content knowing that Rubeus and I are synchronised in our sleeping patterns. I get out of bed and go through to the bathroom to fill my glass of water up. As I flick the light switch on, nothing happens. I flick it again, and still, nothing happens. I go to put one of the lamps in the bedroom on, but it doesn't work either. I check the phone charger, and it's not working. I hope this isn't a power cut. I remember reading that the fuse box was in the storage cupboard in the utility room. I wake Graham up, and we head down using the torch on our phones as light. We get downstairs, Rubeus inquisitively tail-gating our every move, and find the fuse box.

"All fixed." Graham sleepily announces.

"Is that it?" I ask, amazed it was that easy.

As if to prove himself a hero, he flicks the utility light on. "That's it." He answers with a wink. "No big deal."

Thank goodness. Something more serious would not have gone down well with me, not on my family weekend. We walk back through the house to return to our slumber, and an icy draft hits us in our tracks. The front door is wide open. For goodness sake, I told Steven to lock that. I hurry over and shut it. I make sure I lock it, and we go back to bed.

All

I wake up. Ouch. Christ, my head. I open my eyes with great strain and see Jackson is still sleeping. I don't remember getting to bed. I don't remember much at all, actually. Wait. Hold on. Ouch.

I walk through to the bathroom and gulp down water until I feel human again. Then, I walk back through and perch myself on the sofa. I didn't think I drank that much. But I genuinely can't remember much of last night at all. Jackson is still sound asleep. He really must have been tired because he's typically up before me.

-

Well, we might be far from civilisation, but we're not far from nature. I am rudely awoken by the loudest bird chirping I have ever experienced in my life. Goodness. A cacophony of tweets echoes in our bedroom, and due to the lack of curtains, I can tell before opening my eyes just how bright it is.

"Steven?" I say while trying to find his body in the bed.

"Yes, Sleeping Beauty?" He answers, and I can tell he has been up for a while.

"Why is it so bright, and loud, and cold?" I moaned while rubbing my eyes and wincing at the pain of the beautiful bruise I had forgotten about on my face. I chuckle to myself, remembering what mum had done to me yesterday. She's crazy.

"Well. It's bright because there are no curtains. It's loud because all the birds in Scotland want us to know they're awake, and you should be too, and it's cold because someone opened the patio doors in the middle of the night and didn't close them." Steven lectured patronisingly.

"I thought I'd closed the door. Sorry." I grumped as I squinted my eyes open and stretched up out of bed.

"That's ok, princess. But it would be best if you got up. Your mum has made breakfast, and everyone is waiting on you." Steven said, leaving me to dress.

Well, I was positive I remembered closing the door. I maybe didn't lock it. I don't know. I throw on Steven's jumper, pull on my jeans, and head through for breakfast. Mum has made bacon and sausage rolls. I could cry. I'm so happy with that choice.

Everyone is in such a good mood at breakfast, and I notice Claire has the biggest smile on her face. I whisper to Steven about telling everyone now, and he looks at me with a worried face. "It's your family, so we can tell them whenever you want, but remember what we had decided before we arrived." He was right. We did decide to tell everyone tomorrow morning if everyone was in high spirits, but it appeared that we couldn't be having a better holiday. Once the whole family is sat at the table, I look at Steven, and he knows I've made my mind up. He rolls his eyes, kisses me and squeezes my hand.

"Can I have everyone's attention, please?" I ask firmly as I stand up at the table.

I didn't expect complete silence, and now I am nervous.

"Yes, sweet pea?" Mum encourages me to speak.

"Steven and I would like to tell everyone something, and we were hesitant to tell you all this weekend." I could see everyone was genuinely interested in what I had to say. "We found out it was confirmed yesterday morning as we have been going through the motions for over a year now." I continue. I look at Steven, and he has an approving smile on his face. "Steven and I are officially on the adoption waiting list, and if all goes to plan, we should have a child by Christmas." I feel overcome with emotion as I finish telling our news, and there is a question in my mind about whether it's the hangover or it is joy, but I fall into Steven's arms.

-

Did I just hear that correctly? I look at Graham, and his eyes have widened in disbelief. We are going to be grandparents. I can't contain my excitement, and I rush over to my boys. I squeeze them both. I'm over the moon for them. Rubeus is jealous of the attention and tries to nuzzle in on the hug. "I'm so happy for you both!" I tell them through tears.

-

Wow. That's crazy. My big brother is going to be a dad. My big brother who is more like a little brother sometimes. My big brother. Kids. This is too much. I'd gotten over the fact that I would be an aunty when Claire was pregnant, but I never really thought about Kyle and Steven having a baby. I see Jackson's facial expression hasn't changed from shocked, and I laugh and nudge him. We get up, and Jackson shakes their hands. I throw my arms around them both. "You are going to make amazing-ly bad parents. I love it!"

"I think you mean you'll be an amazing-ly bad aunt!" Kyle countered.

-

A child by Christmas? That was Mike and I's dream. I feel a pang in my stomach. I stand and walk up the stairs to the bedroom. I have carried the blanket mum wrapped us in as babies with me since Mike, and I lost ours. Kyle and Steven deserve it. I pull it out of my bag and carry it downstairs. I thought I'd feel empty at this moment, but I feel great. I'm excited for the boys. They'll be perfect parents. So will Mike and I. When the time is right. I come back into the dining area, and Kyle catches my eye. I give him the blanket and pull him into a hug.

Kyle

I was still floating on cloud nine after telling the family our news and receiving all the support, especially from Claire. I couldn't wipe the smile off my face. It was as though telling the family made it real. Steven and I are going to be dads. My heart skipped a beat, and I was bouncing around the bedroom, getting ready to go fishing with dad and Mike.

I hate fishing but dad loves it. He always tried to force an interest out of me when I was younger, and it never came, but I immensely enjoy just sitting with him out on the boats, so I continue to go along annually. Luckily, Mike likes fishing as well - or at least has the knowledge to converse with dad on the subject.

I remember once, when we were kids, dad took us all fishing. The weather wasn't ideal, and Claire just point-blank refused to get out of the car at all. I was wearing wellie boots that kept getting stuck in the mud, and because I hate being dirty, I burst into tears. On the other hand, Ellie loved the weather and the dirt, but rather than take an interest in dad's fishing skills; she consistently jumped into the muddy river requiring immediate saving due to the current of the brook's strength having superiority over Ellie's swimming skills. Dad drove us home that night a shell of the man he is. We were never told off for our behaviour, but dad never took us fishing again.

It was only a few years ago I asked if I could start joining his little jaunts into the water. Not just to escape reality but to spend some quality time with my pops.

I am standing at the patio doors in our bedroom, waiting on Mike and dad, looking out to the gorgeous view that I've still not gotten over, and I notice there are footprints on the crisp frosted snow. That's highly unsatisfying. It must have been someone when they walked Rubeus. Or Jackson when he went for a run. Actually, yes, it would have been Jackson. No one in this family would do that. We're all a bit anal when it comes to order and neatness; thanks to mum for passing on her irrationalities to us all.

Dad appears outside the patio doors and frightens me. I can feel how excited he is. Bless him. I find it amusing how much he enjoys fishing. Holding a stick with a bit of string on the end in the hope of catching a slimy and smelly fish. I just don't get it. But he loves it, so I don't need to understand. I used to think he just liked the peace away from mum, and to be fair, that reason is probably still very valid.

I feel like Mike had a similar upbringing to us in that his dad also tried to force fishing on him, the only difference being his dad succeeded. I don't think he fishes with anyone apart from dad. His dad passed before he met Claire, so I presume he only goes fishing to feel closer to him. He often talks about him and how he would have loved us all.

As we make our way down the garden path towards the loch, it's not as cold as it looks. The grass is frosted but is on the cusp of melting, and there doesn't appear to be any ice plates on the water. However, the birds are still incessantly twittering in the woods, and there's a thick quilt of grey clouds above. The cloud density is probably why the temperature isn't too low.

We walk down to the little jetty, which does not look or feel secure enough for the three of us to be stood on it. Mike pulls in the fishing boat that has drifted off ever so slightly into the loch, and as he does so, ripples scatter across the still water. It's just a tiny fishing boat. How all three of us will get in is still a mystery to me. As it gets closer, I notice the ripples are becoming slightly more aggressive, and by the time the boat reaches the jetty, it has half sunk: sitting like a shipwreck in the shallow end of the loch.

I turn to dad, who looks devastated. I burst out laughing, and Mike joins in with a chuckle too.

"I checked the boat yesterday. It was fine." Dad looked from Mike to me, confused.

"You sure, Dad? The bottom of the boat looks pretty destroyed."

"Positive. I checked after we arrived. The boat was in perfect condition."

"Well, something has attacked the bottom of the boat in the night." Mike offered, inspecting the boat further. "It's as if the bottom has been slightly damaged over time, and then something has jumped into it with a lot of force. Or. Someone has come at it with a jackhammer." Mike offered the latter part of his explanation with a chortle.

Dad isn't happy but agrees with Mike's suggestion to walk a bit around the loch to where the water is deeper to cast his line. Furthermore, after not even ten minutes after having pitched up and sat down, dad's smile is back. Mike pulls out three bottles of beer from the ice box, and I find myself looking back at the lodge. It really is a stunning building. A modern hideaway in the middle of nature. Like mother nature bejewelled. I definitely feel like it needs to be on an episode of grand designs. I can see Claire in the upstairs lounge, staring out at the landscape. I give her a wave, but she doesn't see us. We are pretty well hidden by the long grass. I can see into every room of the house, actually. Mum and Steven are in the downstairs lounge, and Ellie is in the kitchen. This is cool. I love people watching. I'm glad we're in the middle of nowhere as I begin to feel voyeuristic after Steven and I's bedtime last night. Wait. This is truly a little weird. I was oblivious to the lodge's and our blazon visibility across the glen. What if there are hill walkers or a really lost dog walker? They'll see us.

"I'm really chuffed for you and Steven, bud." Mike attracted my attention away from the looming alarm of being seen from all angles of the glen.

"Thank you. We are over the moon, obviously. We were a bit nervous to tell everyone because we didn't want to upset you or Claire." I offer still hesitant in case I cause offence.

"There's no way you've upset me, mate. On the contrary, I'm ecstatic for the both of you. Truly. Plus, after last night, I don't think Claire will be upset for a long time. If you know what I mean." Mike said, finishing it with a wink. He loves a wink.

"That's my sister!" I exclaim. I don't want to hear about their sex life. Dad lets out a chuckle. "Dad!"

"But in all seriousness, we are both happy for you. You both deserve it." Mike said genuinely.

"Aye, you both really do, son. I'm so proud of you all."

"Stop it, you guys! No sign of toxic masculinity here." I joke.

"Plus, judging by Claire's mood this morning, we might have two little nippers on next year's holiday." Dad offered innocently.

"We'll take it one step at a time, Graham! Thank you very much." Mike joked. "That's the dream though. That is the dream." Mike drifted off and looked toward Claire, who was painting in the upstairs lounge.

"Cousins and best friends. Too cute." I say before thinking about how badly Ellie would take to that. She loves being the baby of the family. She might like the idea of being a cool aunt, but only time will tell if she likes it in reality.

As the day drifts on and the likelihood of dad catching anything dwindles, the beautiful and plush grey quilt that cloaked the sky becomes a dark, gloomy graphite grey and has lowered to hide the upper halves of the surrounding hills. It's a wonderfully eerie vista. Through the wood, beyond the loch that follows the two-mile long driveway, comes a distant fog that is low-lying and entwining itself around the trees. Before long, it will have engulfed the wood entirely. I think it's beautiful when a mist lies on the water. I hope it carries on out of the wood and glides over the loch.

"I think we are going to have to admit defeat soon, Graham." Mike interrupted the silence. "That fog is advancing in on us fast and thick."

"Fast and thick, eh?" Dad asks cheekily with a chuckle.

"You need to stop." I demand. Although I find it quite funny when mum or dad talk about sex, I like it to remain ever so slightly taboo. That way, it continues to be funny and packs a punch.

Nonetheless, we all agree to pack up and head back to the lodge.

Shelley

The boys have just left to go fishing, and I spy Claire bringing her paints in from the car. Oh, I'm ever so glad she's brought them with her. She's always been an outstanding painter. She has painted numerous paintings that are on show around Scotland, and when she was little, her drawings were always entered into competitions. As a whole family, we once went to London, where Claire came third in the young painter of the year competition. I think she would have pursued a career in painting had it not been for the lack of stability which would not have done Claire any good, what with her thirst for order and regiment.

Steven, the charming man he is, has requested to accompany me on a walk through the wood with my little Rubeus. He's waiting for me at the door while I attempt to put Rubeus's lead on.

"Do you think he'll need that, Shell?" Steven asks.

"I just don't want him to run out onto the road."

"Luckily, the road is two miles away, so I think you can give him a pass on the lead today!"

I suppose that is true. He never strays too far away from me anyway. Rubeus is quite satisfied when I give up trying. He hates wearing his lead, but he also thinks that if he barks at a car, it will stop for him, so I like him to wear it to be safe. Walks at home have become a rarity because he wrestles so much with his lead, and we have had to gate and fence our entire back garden to keep him in. Not because he'd run away but because he likes to meet everyone and everything within his vicinity: be it human, dog, car or shadow.

I throw my coat on, and we head outside.

"Oh no, look, someone has walked over the beautiful white lawn." That's saddening. I like it when things are tidy.

"Well, it definitely wasn't me." Steven defends himself before I lay blame.

"It was probably Jackson. He's the only one who would do that; bless him. He's not tidy like us. Yet!" I joke.

As we walk down the garden path, along the thin strip next to the cars, and before we reach a little opening to the woods, I can see the boys plodding along the edge of the loch. I thought there was a boat they were going to use. I'm sure Graham mentioned a boat yesterday.

"Are we going left or right, Shell?" Steven asks, having reached two entrances, one on either side of the road.

Right is thin and just curves around the loch and leads to hills. Left is vast and dense, curving around half the parameter of the lodge and stretching for as far as the eye can see. I think we'll go right to get a better view of the lodge, loch: and no road in sight to be on the safe side with Rubeus.

"Right." I announce before leading the way.

Before long, we are lost in the throng of the trees. Deep in conversation about children, politics and religion. Essentially we have been putting the world to rights. I love chatting with Steven because he is very worldly. His opinions always have gravitas, and he always remains respectful in debates and discussions. I would never tell anyone, but Steven is definitely my favourite son-in-law. I love Mike and Jackson, don't get me wrong, but Steven is very logical and level-headed: I feel like I can talk to him about anything.

"Claire seems to be in high spirits this weekend." I put forward as the topic of our next conversation.

"She does. I think this is exactly what she needs. It probably didn't help that she threw herself back into work or that Mike did exactly the same thing." Steven reasoned.

"Absolutely." I agree. "They never made time to mourn or re-bond as a couple." I throw Rubeus's stick for him.

"Couple time is underrated in modern society. We have friends who spend the majority of their lives apart from their partners. Kyle and I barely survive work without seeing each other. We have to speak with each other every other hour, or we lose focus."

Rubeus returns with a new stick, clearly having found a better one and decided it was Steven's time to throw.

"Graham and I are exactly the same, and I would like to think we've instilled that in our three."

"Thinking about it as well, not being able to check in with social media is a heavenly detox. Claire's work, or her friends, are unable to distract her from her marriage and her family out here."

I knew Steven would have logical thoughts on Claire.

"It's just a pity you're all in different cities." I say, manoeuvring around a suspicious brown patch.

"Ellie often comes through to see us in Edinburgh. I think more as free accommodation to see her friends from university, and we do meet up with Claire and Mike every few weeks." Steven offers, trying to appease my apparent upset. "Plus, we've all said once we have children, we'll be moving closer to home."

Steven's family are from the next town over to us, which is perfect. We've become good friends over the years, so luckily, we don't get cut short on birthdays and at Christmas. Unfortunately, Mike's parents have both passed, which is sad for him but good in the selfish respect that they will nest closer to us when the time comes. Ellie and Jackson, however, are still a mystery. They've been together a year and a half but don't appear to have marriage on their minds, and I can't see them settling down with careers any time soon. Also, we've never actually met Jackson's parents. All we know is that he is from the countryside.

"I'm happy she's happy. Hopefully, it has been put behind her for good now."

"Agreed." Steven says with an affectionate squeeze of my shoulder.

I genuinely am hopeful her depression won't return. There's no way I could ever burden her with my illness while she is in a rut like that. Oh goodness. I'd forgotten all about my condition.

"Rubeus?" Steven calls out. "Haven't seen him for a minute. He's probably terrorising some poor squirrel or something." He jokes.

We walk a little quicker, looking around us, and I spot the little white fluff ball in the distance playing with something. As we approach closer, I can see that he's playing with something material and blue. Where on earth would he have found that? Finally, Rubeus notices our impending arrival and pulls his treasure over to show us. He is savagely biting into what now appears to be the remains of a sleeping bag.

"Where has he got that from?" Steven asked, looking around for more evidence as to the sleeping bag's origin.

I genuinely had no idea. I pulled it out of Rubeus's mouth, folded it as small as I could, and squeezed it into a bag I had in my pocket. I always have a plethora of supermarket bags in my pocket for unscheduled constitutionals. Rubeus wasn't happy, but I knew he'd eat the bag's insulation, and it would upset his tummy, so I put it in the bag to put in the bin on our return.

"Shell!" Steven called me over. He'd followed the route of the sleeping bag, like Hansel and Gretel with pieces of it strewn in a path to a tiny clearing in the wood.

The clearing was very small and circular in shape. There was an indication of a dead campfire in the centre and imprints in the ground like bodies had laid around for a while, perhaps overnight.

"You don't think someone would come this far away from civilisation to camp for the night?" I asked Steven, wanting him to say no.

"Well, the evidence suggests so, Shell. There's a bag over there with some rubbish in it. Empty cans and crisp packets." Steven explained. "It looks like a couple of people camped out at some point and didn't take some of their rubbish or their sleeping bag home with them."

I was still not happy they'd come this far, but I reasoned myself to accept the facts. The campfire was a little black hole in the centre of the clearing made of twigs and a newspaper. A newspaper! I rush over to check the date of the newspaper, but there's nothing left of it. If the fire crackled throughout the night, then nothing would be left of the paper. Something about me just doesn't like this. It doesn't feel right. Anyway. I'm probably just overthinking things.

Once Rubeus is quite done with his demolition and destruction of the derelict camp, he dictates to move on. Steven appears to be confident in our location within the wood, which I am glad of. If I were alone, the only way I'd see out for myself would be the hope of a rescue mission. Nevertheless, we are plundering on through the depths of this deceivingly dense wood. Thank goodness we chose the smaller segment. After a short time, I begin to recognise clearings and patches of nature on the path back to the lodge. However, there is a rather ominous fog stalking our trail, pulling with it an icy breath that sends a shiver down my back.

We can see the loch now through the trees, and I can see the lodge in the clearing up ahead. The fog appears to have descended from the hills and is currently spreading across the loch. It is a beautiful sight.

As soon as we get into the lodge, I put the heating up. Steven and I are freezing, and the boys will be just as bad from fishing all day.

Ellie

"What do you want to do today?" I playfully ask Jackson as he helps me make the bed by ruffling the covers each time he lays them flat.

"Would you stop, please?" He asked, giving me an angry look while holding back a laugh. "I'm not bothered. I want to go for another run at some point." He said while smoothing the bed for a final time and shooing me away, then sitting himself on the sofa in our room with his book.

I kiss him before going to get washed and dressed. The water pressure is excellent. There is nothing better than a powerful shower. A powerful shower has the ability to clear your mind and help you rationalise whatever is going on in your life. Any issues or problems I face are always reasoned with and solved in the shower. Or a bath. I'm not prejudiced against either. I've always just been a water baby. I can't remember why but mum used to take me swimming every morning before school as a child. We'd get up before everyone else in the house and have our mother-daughter bonding time in the car. Then she'd sit at the side of the pool and read her book or eat her breakfast while I'd swim. I would swim laps until I was tired or until mum called me. Sometimes if I did get tired before time was up, I'd just bomb at the deep end. I don't know if mum knew it, but being in the pool really helped clear my mind. I looked forward to it. I'd go to school level-headed and fresh-eyed. When I was getting bullied, it was my outlet to release the anger and pain but also my space to get over what was happening. When I was sitting my exams, it was my study space. Everything made sense after I'd been in the water.

Today was no exception. I was struggling with something that I learned only last week, and I'd hoped Kyle had pushed me to tell him last night: but he didn't. Kyle was my second port of call if I didn't have access to water in order to clear my mind. However, he might not be so impartial with his advice on the matter.

As I am stood in the shower with the water hitting my back, I recall how a friend had contacted me last weekend with something to tell me. I had her come round that night as I sensed an urgency in her tone. She arrived and seemed agitated, and for most of her visit, I questioned if she was comfortable or confident enough to divulge the information that had prompted her call. She asked me how I was. She asked me how the family was. She asked me how mum was. Why was she asking about them? Why was she asking questions and not telling me why she was here? I was beginning to get agitated and impatient, so I asked her.

What she told me knocked me back, and I was left speechless. Surely she was joking. She wasn't.

How should one react when they hear their mum may have cancer?

Apparently, it had been malignant, but they had caught it in time, and it was now dormant. Mum is now in remission. My friend is a nurse and has been the one to take mum's blood tests. She said before she left that it was a significant security breach her telling me, but she thought I should know.

I had no idea what to do with the information I had been given. Clearly, mum and dad weren't ready to tell us: presuming dad knew in the first place. Should I bring it up with mum? Should I mention it to Kyle or Claire? Would Jackson be able to rationalise my thoughts? What happens if the cancer isn't dormant? What would we do if something happened to mum?

All of these questions had been playing on my mind for over a week. I was furious my so-called friend had seen fit to tell me. I suppose she might not have if the test results had come back negative. I believe it should have been mum's responsibility to say to me when she felt ready. Did mum even know her test results? Did she know she had the all clear?

With the shower massaging me and the warmth invigorating my senses, I reasoned to keep quiet about what I knew, to forgive my friend for doing what she thought was best and not to push mum's buttons too much. Then, when mum was ready, she would talk to us. She knows we are all here for her, and she knows how much we love her.

I turn the shower off, feeling like a weight has been lifted after spending focused time going over everything in my head. Jackson is still in the same position on the sofa, reading his book.

"Good shower?" He asks knowingly, without looking up.

"Perfect." I said whole-heartedly.

"I will go out running once I've finished this chapter."

"Ok. I'll probably just putter around the house." I wanted to explore all of the lodge's nooks and crannies.

"You're good at puttering." Jackson said with a wink as he got up and got changed into his running gear.

As I dried and straightened my hair, I took my time, waiting for Jackson to leave. He doesn't like me being nosey and most likely would disapprove of my prying around the lodge. So I followed him up the stairs and saw him out before beginning my expedition. I started upstairs, passing Claire and the sacred easel as I snuck into her room. I don't think she even noticed me.

I couldn't believe Claire and Mike had never made their bed. Mum would be displeased. Actually. I'm displeased. Before I started opening cupboard doors, I found myself unapologetically and compulsively making their bed. Once I was satisfied, I rifled through the room. Their room was much nicer than ours. Their bathroom was palatial. The bath is literally on a platform. I am not finding anything interesting in here, so I walk back through the lounge and into mum and dad's room. Their room is a little smaller but just as cosy and modern. The wardrobes in mum's room are attractive. They've been hand built into a corner space in the room. Nothing is stimulating here. I head downstairs and continue my search. I am fascinated and slightly puzzled by the tiny cupboard which houses a mop and a broom just off the utility room. Why would someone build this stunning house and make this minuscule cupboard? I'm slowly beginning to get bored. When I open all of the cubbyholes on the ground floor, all I find is a draft, so I head down to the basement rooms. Obviously, there's still the mystery of whatever is in the blocked off room and why the boiler sounds like it is breathing. I press my ear to the door and can't hear a thing today. It could be because the heating isn't on yet. The only cupboard left for me to find something interesting is the cupboard in the games room. It's locked, I remember, so I grab my tool kit and pick the lock. Again, a loud and clear click signals my success. I excitably swing open the door.

Finally. Something more than cold air and cleaning products.

The first thing I pull out is a sleeping bag. Bog standard. Below the sleeping bad is a rucksack which appears to be filled with something. A box of matches. Always handy. Three torches. Three ropes. Three scarves. Three balaclavas. Three is the magic number. A bottle of vodka. The magic drink. A bottle of something ambiguous. Possibly less magical. Then in the front pocket, I pull out a plethora of knives; flick knives, daggers, hunting knives and a cleaver. Beneath the rucksack filled with goodies is a box packed with more ropes and tapes.

The owners are wild. They must like camping, which explains why they would have a lodge in the middle of nowhere. Or doesn't.

Not entirely satisfied with my findings, I retire to lie on my bed. I like being nosey. I'm dropping in and out of a nap: I can't believe how sleepy I am. I must be relaxed. I cuddle up on the plush covers and allow myself to drift off.

I can feel my cheek sitting on a damp puddle on the cushion. I drooled. I roll over and notice that Jackson is in the room. I'm surprised he never woke me up. My eyes feel dry, and I feel heavy. HOPEFULLY, if I stay on the bed, he'll come over for a cuddle. I drift back into a peaceful nap.

I wake suddenly to Jackson closing the bedroom door. He's never been subtle.

"Are you napping?" He asks, raising his eyebrow, giving me a mischievous grin.

"Only a little." I answer, stretching out, trying to be cute. "How long have I been asleep?"

"Pass. I'm just back."

"Are you?" I ask, slightly bewildered, before a warm and sweaty top gets thrown on my face.

"I'm sure I woke up at one point and saw you."

"Nope. You must be dreaming about me, Elle." Jackson winked as he finished undressing and walked naked to the bathroom. God, I love his body. "Pity you've done your hair already today. You could have joined me in the shower. I'm pretty hot and sweaty."

I can do my hair again.

Claire

"Did you mention the shower situation to Kyle or Steven?" Mike asked, drying himself off with his towel. I still wasn't quite used to seeing him naked again, and I felt like a schoolgirl as my heart quivered with temptation.

"Absolutely not. I'll laugh it off if they bring it up, but I just want to forget about it." I cringed, recalling my pathetic attempts at seduction from yesterday.

"Would it not be better just to clear the air and laugh it off if you bring it up?" Mike offers.

"No." Just let me forget it. "What if it was Steven, not Kyle, and then I bring it up to Kyle?" I shivered at the thought.

Mike began to laugh. "It genuinely won't matter. They would both find it funny."

"We'll see." I'm on a high, and I don't want anything to knock me down.

I believe this excellent mood is impenetrable. I haven't had this clarity of mind for months.

"What are your plans for today?" Mike asks as he kisses me and heads towards the door.

"I think I'm going to go and grab my paints." I answer, which stops Mike dead in his tracks.

"Are you serious?" He excitably asks.

"Yes. I want to. I really want to. I'm going to sit in the upstairs lounge and paint the glen."

Mike comes back to me and squeezes me. He'd convinced me to pack my paints; with the logic that if I forced myself to paint, I might force myself out of my depression. It's madness to think that just twenty-four hours ago, I never thought I'd be happy again. I never thought I'd smile or bear the thought of Kyle getting a baby. I never thought I'd have sex with Mike ever again. But. Here I am, walking down the stairs with a smile on my face, thinking about becoming an aunt and still tingling from last night.

Mike had packed the car, and I laugh as I open the boot. He has packed my entire ream of canvas paper instead of just a few sheets. He has packed my entire paint collection, not just a select palate. He has even packed my easel. Bless him.

I carry what I need up the stairs and plant myself in the corner of the upstairs lounge with a view of the vista of the glen. My eye is caught and helps with the surfeit of greens and greys. I love working in a palette of shades rather than primary colours. A few years ago, I'd won a competition for a piece I'd painted in a zoo. The theme had been animals in art, and my painting of Norris, the elephant, had managed to win Mike and me a trip to Florida, where I had to attend select art shows and provide paintings for my own exhibition. We were out there for three weeks and managed to do all the sights. All the parks. It was a magical holiday. We were even treated like celebrities with a chauffeur service for our entire visit. My exhibition opened on our penultimate night out there, and I had managed to provide another five new paintings to join Norris the elephant, as well as a few from my already existing portfolio. It was then that I found my voice as an artist. I was seeing the light and dark in animate, or inanimate, shapes with undistinguished hues. The most successful piece I did was of a flamboyance of flamingos at dusk, which was at that exhibition in Florida and sold for thousands. It actually bought Mike and I's car. The surplus of pink, salmon, peach, cerise, maroon, pastel pink, baby pink and violet really tickled my artistic senses.

I'd always wanted to paint full time. I managed to earn quite a bit of money over the years. Enough for a good few holidays, our car and a big chunk of our mortgage deposit. But not enough for a consistent living wage. Mike always promised I could quit my job and paint full time if he got promoted, but he continually appeared to get passed over for promotions.

I am sitting here, mixing different shades of greens and greys to capture the richness of our surroundings, and I allow myself to get lost in the canvas. I allow myself the complete onus to shut out every extraneous sound. I allow my senses to focus solely on sight and touch. I am seeing the landscape and my colours. I am feeling the brush in my hand, and the paint skate across the canvas.

Something pulls me out of my bubble. Did I hear something? I pop my head from behind my easel. No one is there. Has everyone left? I think I'm alone. Sometimes, if I have been painting all day, I will not have noticed Mike leave for, and return from work until he comes through to the study to tell me dinner is ready. I used to feel slightly guilty for losing hours and sometimes days, but I have come to accept the painting as my outlet in life, and I embrace these times when I can lose myself in the art. If it isn't already, it helps to clear my mind.

Towers of teal and juts of jade reach up to graze the low-lying billows of grey that fill the skyline like a lavish quilt smothering the ground. A stretch of crystal grey has a muffled glisten and runs concentrically with the tumbling emerald knolls that fill the majority of the panorama. Curves in shades of moss and lime pile and overpower one another, overlapping in no apparent pattern and hiding the horizon from view. A graphite tone hangs above the lavish mushroom quilt, which drops into an ivory mist sandwiched on the horizon.

Again, something pulls me out of my bubble. I feel like I heard something again. It's probably someone in the lodge. I listen intently but can't hear anything else. The light outside is fading faster than I'd have liked it to, but I think I'm done with my painting anyway. I slowly put my things away and touch up my work as I do. I am rather proud of this piece, actually. I'll gift it to mum and dad. Once I've tidied everything away, I put the painting in our room to dry and go to clean the brushes in the bathroom sink.

Our bed is made. That's weird. I don't remember making it. It scares me when I don't remember doing things because my subconscious autopilot has taken over and steered my body to do as it modally would do. I often find myself parked in the driveway, having driven home from work, and I can't for the life of me remember leaving work, let alone any of the drive home.

I head downstairs for a glass of water and get comfortable on the sofas where I can see the boys fishing. I wonder why they are on the bank rather than in the boat. I close my eyes.

All

"I think we have enough, Kyle." Steven warned as I crammed the fourth bottle of wine into my jeans pockets.

"There is never enough wine, baby. Plus, you don't know how long we will be down there." I retort with sass.

"I'm sure someone can make the treacherous expedition all the way up the stairs for another bottle or two if the unimaginable happens and we run out of wine downstairs."

"I love you." I say to Steven with forceful a kiss to shut him up.

"Are you trying to make me quiet?"

How did he know?

"No..." I'll change the subject. "Anyway. We have Mario kart in the bag, but we need a second place for darts and pool to be in with the chance of winning overall."

"Yes, dear. I'll try."

"Don't try, do." I joke.

We are constructing a games extravaganza downstairs and want to make sure there is enough wine for the entirety of the event. In teams of two, each group must choose a player to play; pool, darts, dominoes and Mario kart. Each player will play every player for each game, and they will be scored four points for first place and one point for fourth place.

-

"I don't even know why you're bothering. You know I'm going to win this one, guys." I say, throwing my first dart without even looking at the board. I felt a pang of nerves after my big words, but I got a triple seventeen and breathed a sigh of relief.

"Fighting talk will only enrage the beast." Claire said with a growl, which makes everyone laugh.

"And what beast would that be, Claire?" I ask with a snort.

My family are very competitive. We've always played games and created our own competitions. Monopoly, scrabble, trivial pursuit, Pictionary; you name it, we have made a champion's league out of it. Nonetheless, I've always been a good shot. I was always good at throwing games at the Christmas markets, and I could always spray the water directly into the holes at theme parks. I guess it's my natural talent. As a result of my aptitude for precision, I ended up with an abundance of knockoff cuddly toys as a teenager. I think mum still has them all in a box in the attic. All my little trophies.

"Come on! Throw, Ellie!" Claire shouted in an aggressive manner.

"Claire!" Mum called her out on her behaviour which made Rubeus jump up from his bemused slumber where he had been lying peacefully.

"Never too old to be told off by mum, Clairy Fairy!" I taunted.

"Never too old for a wedgie, Ellie Bean." Claire jibed right back, slightly under her breath, so mum didn't hear.

-

Graham was the most competitive person I'd ever met when I was younger. It's actually what attracted me to him initially. I had been brought up with ambition, with a drive to be the best person I could be, and I had never met anyone with such a similar outlook to myself until Graham came along: and we hadn't met anyone quite so aggressively competitive as us until our children became aware of the concept of winning.

With age, I've learnt to conserve my competitive nature for the moments when it really matters. I feel fiercely competitive that I will beat this cancer, for example. However, with family, I'm not particularly eager to beat them too hard. They are my babies, after all.

"Come on, Graham! Don't let your daughter beat you. You show them who the real daddy is!" I yell for moral support as Graham navigates his way around the world of Mario and Luigi in Princess Peach's limousine.

"Mum, that sounded a little dirty." Ellie pointed out as she, too, drove over the mushroom race track.

"And what, Ellie, does your dad and I's dirty talk put you off your game?" I ask cheekily to a response of laughter.

"Your dad and I love to have sex."

"MUM!" Ellie squirms.

"We've had sex. At least three times, you know."

"MUM! STOP!" Ellie cries, and Graham jumps up and cheers as he crosses the finish line just before Ellie.

Whoops. I may have forgotten my own rules there.

-

Steven is going down.

As a teenage girl at university, with long blonde hair and confidence by the bucket load, I was always getting asked on dates. I would, of course, accept: on one condition, that we went to the snooker rooms. Of course, they would think they were in for a treat, teaching innocent little Claire how to play, but what would surprise those poor unsuspecting boys is my propensity for snooker. All those dates of practice were leading me to this. Beating all those educated, try-hard teenage boys had got me to now.

"I'm going to annihilate you, Stevie boy. You don't know who you're dealing with." I affront Steven.

"Please, don't embarrass yourself, Claire!" Steven says calmly, ending it with a wink before taking his first shot.

This game decides the winner and second place. We only had dominoes left, and Kyle and Steven were in the lead. I have to win this for Mike and me. I'm playing for spots, and Steven is playing for stripes. It certainly was a tense game, and Mike and Kyle gave very little support. They probably knew it was pointless. I am going to win.

I have to hand it to Steven; he plays a good game. A ball is potted on each turn. "You're fighting a losing battle, mate!" I can't let him know I think he's good. He'll use that against me.

We are both going for the black ball now. How did we get to here? I can't believe he's my equal. I can't let him win. I can't let all my experiences go to waste.

I play my turn to put the black ball right against the table's edge. There's no way Steven will be able to pot it from there. He doesn't. He forces the black ball right into the middle of the table in a perfect position for...me...to...pot...it. Success.

-

We hadn't won an overall game yet, so it all came down to me. We had won at dominos. At least then, we would be in with a chance of winning overall. I wasn't too sure where the scores laid at the minute. They don't matter. All that matters is this game of dominos I am playing against Mike.

"You ready?" Mike asked.

I didn't answer. Instead, I picked a domino from the side. Double five. Excellent. Mike picks a two-four. I play first.

"Well done, my darling. Keep calm and think about every move." Graham was rubbing my back as I played.

"Excuse me, no inter-team physical contact until the games are over, thank you very much." Kyle shooed Graham off my back.

"That's the problem with competing against your children. The students have become the masters." Claire added.

Graham and I used to implement a technique of squeezing each other to help when playing games. I say used to; we were definitely going to attempt to utilise the method now; if Kyle hadn't called us out. We used to squeeze once for yes, twice for no, and if it were multiple choice, the squeezes would resemble the order of answers. Our big mistake was sharing all of our tips and tricks with our children. It made them almost unbeatable. Almost.

"Chapping." Mike said with a furrowed brow.

"It's okay, babe. There is no stress." Claire comforted Mike with her words, sounding somewhat unhinged.

We were both down to our last domino and were both chapping. We each had to pick one up. The room was tense. It felt as though no one was breathing. I was so focused that I could hear Mike turning a domino between his fingers. I could feel everyone staring at us or the table, frozen like a tableau of excited tension.

As I decided how to lay in my head, that's when we heard it. Like a choreographed movement, all nine of us tilted our heads to the ceiling. What was that?

"Did everyone hear that?" Steven whispered.

A shot of adrenaline bolted through me. It was probably because it was a release of tension to move and a frightening thought to bear.

"I think so." Graham whispered in response.

-

I wish mum would hurry up and make her move. I can't breathe. I can't be the one to break this silence, but I also don't want to pass out from self-asphyxiation.

What was that? Like a choreographed movement, all nine of us tilted our heads to the ceiling. But, seriously, what was that?

"Did everyone hear that?" Steven whispered.

A shot of adrenaline bolted through me. It was probably because I took a breath in as I moved in a release of tension and because it sounded like someone was upstairs.

"I think so." Graham whispered in response.

Slowly we all looked at each other almost for reassurance that we were all on the same page. What I'd heard was almost like a floorboard creak, which was odd in itself as I didn't recall any creaky floorboards throughout the lodge. It could have been anything. I open my mouth to sigh in relief and laugh, but it happens again. This time it was louder. This time it appears to have travelled. This time Rubeus wasn't happy. This time my stomach turned.

"Are we being silly?" Kyle asked in a hushed voice.

"Well, why don't I go and inspect?" Jackson heroically offers.

"Are you serious?" I ask him.

"Of course. We are probably getting spooked by the heating system or something. But I'll go and inspect." He said, picking up a snooker cue and smiling at us all.

"I'll come with you." Steven offered, picking up the other snooker cue.

"Don't be silly." Jackson said to Steven, waving at him to stay.

"I'll cover the stairs at least, then."

"Okay."

They both leave in a silent creep.

-

"Well, pass me the wine." I say, grabbing the last two bottles of wine from the bar top.

"Fill me up too." Claire said as she thrust her glass into my face.

"Fill us all up, darling." Mum said with a slight quiver in her voice before picking up Rubeus for a cuddle. Bless her; she must have got a fright.

"Should we finish our game?" Mike asks mum.

"Yeah, you should. Stay calm and carry on, and all that jazz." I say with a cheers to the room.

As mum lays her penultimate domino and Mike lays his, the thirst for tension and our competitive nature force us to forget the noises we heard and that two of us were out investigating. Finally, mum allows her poker face to drop for just a moment, and she lets slip a cheeky smile. She's beautiful. She takes a deep breath before laying her final domino.

What is that? Like a choreographed movement, all seven of us tilted our heads to the ceiling. But, seriously, what is that?

"Did everyone hear that?" Claire whispered. "Do you think it's the boys?"

A shot of adrenaline bolted through me. Probably because I remembered my husband could be battling off intruders with a snooker cue right now.

"I think so." Graham whispered in response.

We all held our focus on the door as we heard footsteps coming down the stairs. There was no chatter. Surely if it were Steven and Jackson, they would be talking? Then, finally, the footsteps reached the bottom of the stairs. We had all held our breath in tense anticipation. Whoever it was had reached the door. I could see the shadow of their boots in the gap below the door. I could feel my heart thumping against my chest. The door handle turned slowly. My eyes watered. I wish I had Steven's hand to hold.

The door swung open, and Jackson and Steven burst through in a fit of laughter.

"Well?" Mum demanded an explanation in a rage at their wind up.

"There's nothing upstairs, Shell. I think it's just the central heating. It's swelteringly hot upstairs, so I switched it off." Jackson eased everyone's minds as he took the cue from Steven and put them both back in their holder on the wall.

Thank goodness. "What did we expect to be up there? We're in the middle of nowhere." I brush off the scare we just had with rationalised humour.

"Exactly. We're in the middle of nowhere. With no signal. No contact with the world. That's what makes it so scary." Claire outlays.

"Christ on a bike, Claire! Back to more important matters...BOOM." Mum says as she lays her final domino and steals the win for her and dad.

-

If Ellie rubs their win in my face once more, I will take her darts and use her as a board. They won the most points overall so were named the champions. We drew for second place with Kyle and Steven, and mum and dad came last. We are all laughing about how we spooked ourselves earlier on, and dad and Mike are getting ready to play Pictionary. Mum, Steven, Kyle and I are sat on the couch watching Mike struggle with the easel.

"I'm so happy you're happy, Claire, darling." Mum said to me, grabbing my attention.

"I'm happy that I'm happy. Believe me." I reply. I'm glad mum has brought my mood up in conversation. "I can see clearly now, and I can see how irrational and selfish I was being."

"No more irrational and selfish than normal, Clairy Fairy!" Kyle jibes before Steven tells him to shut up.

"I am sorry, guys."

"Don't be sorry, baby girl." Mum comforts me. "It's completely understandable. I'm just over the moon; you found your way out of the dark tunnel and back into Mike's arms."

I am engulfed by the three of them as they cuddle me, and I feel like this is the perfect time for me to bring up the shower thing with the boys.

"I'm also completely embarrassed and sorry for what I said when I was in the shower yesterday."

Steven gave me a blank stare and looked from Kyle to mum in order to see who I was directing my comment to. So it definitely wasn't him.

"What do you mean, sweetness?" Mum inquired.

"Well, when I was in the shower yesterday, I thought Mike came in, and I was talking to him, but it turns out it wasn't him, so it must have been Kyle." I ended with a laugh to make sure they knew I wasn't cross.

"Wasn't me, Claire." Kyle shunned the idea.

I bet he's winding me up. He wants me to embarrass myself further. Fine. I'm not embarrassed. I have had a bottle of wine, and I'm over what happened.

"It was you, Kyle. Stop trying to embarrass me. You're the only other person it could have been."

"I promise you, Claire. I haven't been in your bathroom." Kyle lied pretty well. "Why was it so embarrassing?"

"It doesn't matter." I smile and wink at Kyle.

"Claire, I'm not lying."

"Okay, Kyle."

Shelley

Pictionary was not a successful venture. I think we were all competed out from the adrenaline-inducing extravaganza that came before. Not to mention the tense fear and stress we were all forced to undergo due to the noisy central heating pipes. I didn't want to stay downstairs if we weren't going to play any more games because it is darker and there is less space to get comfy, nor is there enough seating for everyone. Therefore, I convinced everyone to come upstairs to the ground floor lounge where we could spread out and relax, and Graham could make everyone some cocktails in the kitchen area. I'm feeling incredibly positive and safe and secure. I might test the water with how the family might react to my illness.

I get comfy in the corner of one of the sofas while Claire alters the lighting throughout the floor to coincide with the mood. We cosy up with Rubeus in between us. Kyle, Steven and Mike curl into a pretzel on the sofa opposite, and Ellie and Jackson take the cuddle chair. An oddly oversized chair that's realistically too small for two people to sit comfortably. Good. It looks like I'll be able to hold council once we are suitably in possession of a special Graham-made cocktail.

Graham, before he retired, worked for an alcohol distribution company. He worked his way up from assistant salesman to the chief buyer. During his time there, he got to try hundreds of different types of drinks, and he was able to travel the world to where some exotic drinks were made and where they originated. He also got to take me with him sometimes, which was a treat in itself. We went to Italy to learn about Ramazotti, Mexico to learn about tequila and Argentina to learn about Pisco, to name but a few. Having an alcohol expert in the family really helped us to live the high life when it came to hosting soirees and educating our children. We were never interested in tasteless and inebriating vodka. Instead, we were intrigued and enjoyed different flavours. Even our wine must be New Zealand Sauvignon Blanc or an Argentinian Malbec.

Since retiring, Graham has continued his love for different alcohols with mixology classes, where he learns how to create new cocktails every week. That, I love. However, as part of the class, he also learned how to flare bottles, and I did not love the perpetual debris of broken bottles on the kitchen floor; therefore; as a result, he has been forbidden from that practice in the house.

He was excited to bring his new equipment to the lodge and practice making cocktails for the kids.

"Is everyone ready to be made into a cocktail?" Graham asks the room, and I feel a flutter in my heart because it brings me joy to see him so excited.

"That sounds painful." Mike jokes.

"It's going to be magic." Graham assures.

As Graham is in the kitchen, I warn everyone to be supportive. He's very good at making cocktails but can often be, with lack for a better turn of phrase, brutally honest when he's had a few drinks. I am slightly nervous to hear how he may describe everyone in his reasoning behind the cocktails. He's already found the perfect cocktail for me. I am a Spiced Mojito. I'm kind, intelligent, and sophisticated with a spicy and exciting thirst for life, but I have a sharp and curious side that is hidden and will come out when pushed. It's humorous to think about, really. It's almost like my eulogy. Perhaps I should request it for my gravestone. Here lies Shelly. She was a Spiced Mojito.

"Ok, first up is Kyle. He's an easy one." Graham announced as he brought Kyle's cocktail through.

"Easy!" Kyle exclaimed.

Graham ignored Kyle's joke and continued. "Kyle is our smiler. He's always happy. Kyle is curious and resourceful and has a natural ability to vindicate. He's handsome, and his personality has gravitas. His cocktail is a Davy Jones. Spiced rum and Amaretto mixed with coke and topped off with a floating cherry." He finished by presenting the drink to Kyle and rushing away to get the next one.

"Well, your dad sure does think a lot of you, doesn't he?" Steven teased.

"Steven is next, and he was a tricky one to create." Graham proclaimed before taking his position in front of Steven in order to introduce the cocktail to the group.

"Steven is a Basilico."

"Sounds dangerous, Graham." Steven said, sitting up on the sofa.

"A Basilico is made by muddling basil and strawberries with Citrus Vodka, pouring over crushed ice and topping off with peach schnapps and a splash of soda water. Steven is down-to-earth and level-headed. He is strong and charismatic and stands by his opinions fervently."

"Compliment. Compliment. Back-handed compliment. Thank you, G Dog!" Steven said as he graciously took the Basilico from Graham as an award.

"Who's next, dad?" Claire shouts through, clearly impatiently waiting for her drink.

"Ellie." Graham says, bringing through a very fancy looking concoction. "Is mysterious, fresh, full of life and rich in experiences. Her bite is just as big as her bark, and she has a penchant for partying all night long. Ellie is an espresso martini."

"Oh, wow, thanks, dad. That's really nice. I wasn't expecting it to be quite so classy." Ellie sat down and was visibly over the moon with her cocktail.

"I definitely would have made you a Harvey Wallbanger." Claire jibed.

"Or a Sex on the Beach." I cheekily add.

"Mum!"

"Oh, I'm sorry, Ellie, baby. I was just joking."

"Jackson is next. A tall, tanned and intriguing young gentleman who is fiercely protective and has a gentle manner. Jackson is a classic Rum Punch."

"I'll take that. Cheers, G."

Bless Graham, he's put so much effort into all of this, and I can see how happy everyone is with their cocktails.

"Claire, my sophisticated and artistic girl. You have an iron heart and have proved you have integrity and style. You pack a punch and will often leave those you encounter with a headache."

"Well, that took a turn, dad."

"Claire, you are a French Martini."

"I love a French Martini!" Mike exclaimed.

"Well, it's perfect then." I laughed, watching Claire scared to try her drink as she sniffed it. "Oh Claire, when have you ever turned your nose up to alcohol."

"Very true." She took a big gulp. "Delicious."

"Mike. You are a junior Godfather. Whiskey, Amaretto, coke and a dash of pineapple juice. Calm, cheerful, honest, reliable and open to the world and all it offers, if a little naïve. That is why you are a Junior Godfather."

Mike bows to graham before taking his drink and tilts his glass in a cheers to the room.

"Everyone happy?" He asks, handing me my Spiced Mojito and sitting down with his Godfather in hand.

A resounding chorus of yes confirmed a job well done, and I watched my love smile before taking a sip of his drink.

"As we are all sufficiently content, I have something I'd like to share." I begin. Graham gives me a look of wonderment, and I place my hand on his leg as a sign that I'm ok. Everything will be ok.

"Something happened quite a few months ago now. That thing very much shook your dad and me up, and it is still currently underway. I want you all to know that we have everything under complete control. I want you to know that I am not looking for anything to change in our relationships. I am not looking for sympathy or attention, or help. Your father and I have discussed everything, and we have plans for every possible outcome. I need you to understand that I am ok. I am feeling very positive, and I am a fighter."

"Mum..." Claire moved closer to me, and I looked around to see a blend of confusion and fear on my family's faces.

"Around a year ago, I had a fall. It was nothing serious, but it did require me to go to the hospital for some tests. The results of the fall were affirmative, and it had no lasting effect on me. Conversely, as an outcome of the tests, the doctors found something else that might be wrong with me. Every week, I had to go to the hospital for tests, blood tests, scans, and screenings. It seemed never-ending. However, what came back was something I was oblivious to and, to be frank, I was ignorant to think would ever happen to me. At the ripe old age of fifty-nine, I was diagnosed with breast cancer."

"Oh, mum!" Kyle immediately rose and rushed over to hug me. Claire joined in, and I noticed she was crying.

I lovingly picked Kyle and Claire off of me, kissed them both and shooed them back to their seats.

"As I said, I do not want sympathy. I...We have been living with this for almost a year now, and there is nothing your father and I can't handle. I have had the operation which has removed the tumour, and I have had three courses of chemotherapy to remove the traces of cancer the tumour may have left behind."

"Why didn't you tell us, mum?" Kyle asks, wiping a tear away from his own eye.

"We decided not to tell you because we didn't know the severity yet. You all had your own problems and struggles in your own lives. We would have told you if it got worse, but everything so far, touch wood, has been successful."

"But you're our mum. We would have done anything you wanted us to." Claire was still fighting back sobs.

"Well, it shouldn't require me getting ill to see more of my family. Plus, I'd probably been living with it for a much longer time, and I seemed to live just fine beforehand. So I didn't; I don't want anything to change."

I feel like a weight has been lifted. I never realised how heavy this had been weighing on my mind. I had always strived to be open and honest with my children, and I guess, on some level, I did feel slightly guilty for not telling them. I am their mother, after all. I hope they don't hold my decision to not tell them against me.

"Your father and I have an appointment next week with the doctor when we will discover the results of the chemotherapy. If it has not been successful and the cancer has grown, then the course of action will probably be more chemotherapy. However, if it has been successful, then this conversation will have been superfluous."

Everyone was quiet. I don't think they had any idea of what to say. Bless them all.

"I hadn't planned to tell you at all this weekend. I had planned on waiting to unearth my results before telling you."

"But what if the results aren't positive, mum?" Kyle asked.

"Then they are not positive, and you can all help me pick out some snazzy bandanas for my melon head."

Everyone laughed at my joke, which made me feel better. They probably laughed as a release of nervous tension. I didn't care. They laughed. They understood. They were not angry. I love them. I let out an enormous sigh of relief and sat back in my seat. I can feel a surge of emotion reach my throat, and my eyes sting from the salty tears that now appear. I need a drink.

"Anyone for another cocktail?" I ask, downing mine and handing the empty glass to Graham with a wink.

Ellie

"As we are all sufficiently content, I have something I'd like to share."

Imagine if mum was going to tell us about her cancer. What would I say? I doubt she will. She would have told us already if she was going to. Poor mum. At least she has dad. Look at the way dad looks at mum; he's so loving and attentive. I spy Jackson in my peripherals and notice his body language is nothing but cold and distant from me. Great. Maybe he's uncomfortable because he doesn't know what mum's going to say. Wait, I don't know what she's going to say. I need to stop phasing out. Back in the room.

"Something happened quite a few months ago now. That thing very much shook your dad and me up, and it is still currently underway."

Oh lord. Maybe she is going to tell us now. I have no idea what I'm going to do. I have no idea how I'm going to react. I haven't prepared for this. I'm going to have to lie to mum. She has always been able to see straight through my lies. It's like a superpower bestowed on mothers at the birth of their children. Even when I wasn't lying, I'd still get questioned. Hold up. Are you being serious, Ellie? You sound like the most selfish human on the planet. Your mum has cancer, and all you can think about is yourself.

"At the ripe old age of fifty-nine, I was diagnosed with breast cancer."

I'm stunned. I'm frozen. I'm speechless. A chill has trickled up my spine, and I feel nauseous. There is immense impact in hearing those words escape your mother's mouth. It was utterly different hearing it from a friend. But when you hear the words dripped in pain and fear masked with blind confidence, there's nothing but vulnerability on display. This pillar of strength who has brought me up with integrity and self-worth is in pain and is scared. How do I help her? She probably wouldn't want help. My eyes fill with tears, and I look round at the room to see everyone is just as shell-shocked as I am.

"Your father and I have an appointment next week with the doctor when we will discover the results of the chemotherapy. If it has not been successful and the cancer has grown, then the course of action will probably be more chemotherapy. However, if it has been successful, then this conversation will have been superfluous."

Well, she's confirmed that she doesn't know the results yet. Now I'm definitely going to have to lie. How did my friend find out so quickly? I suppose if she were there while the tests were being carried out, she would see. But why has mum not been in to find out yet? Especially since the results are positive and the cancer is in remission, then why wouldn't they just tell her? Why would they force someone to live in a mix of anxiety and sorrow when they could very easily give her a rather swift phone call and make her happy?

"But what if the results aren't positive, mum?" Kyle asked.

"Then they are not positive, and you can all help me pick out some snazzy bandanas for my melon head."

That's hilarious. Mum does have a melon head. But the results are positive, so she won't need to be flashing that bad boy anyway.

"Anyone for another cocktail?" Mum asked, downing her drink and handing the empty glass to dad. "I don't want to hear another word about me or the big C. Do you all hear me?"

"Absolutely." I concur as everyone else nods in agreement.

Dad rushes about collecting in everyone's glasses and leaves to make another round. I never fully appreciated my papa as a child, but now, everything he does melts my heart as an adult. We used to have blazing arguments that bubbled and festered over my teenage years because I couldn't understand why Kyle and Claire had freedom and responsibility and money when I did not. What I forgot, however, is that they are older than I am, and of course, they were going to have and be able to do more than I did while I was younger. Dad was never entirely to blame. I think because Claire and Kyle had been such angels, he didn't have much patience when it came to my behaviour as he expected me to be just like them. Possibly another underlying issue of our battles.

Nevertheless, my papa and I have never had a better relationship than we do now. Since I've stopped being a selfish brat, and dad has calmed and mellowed to accept any imperfect behaviours I may display. To be fair...he probably gave up, thinking I was a lost cause.

Dad returned with another cocktail for everyone and informed us of the lack of remaining alcohol.

"I'll nip into town and pick some up. I've only had a few." Jackson announced, which shocked me as he's never typically so forthright for helping. Perhaps he wants to get drunk.

"Are you sure you're ok to drive?" Mum asked, being her usual worrisome self.

"Definitely. I've only had a few." He smiles before going to get his coat and shoes.

"It had to be you or Jackson because your car is at the back, and the only way to get out of here is to reverse all the way down that road." Kyle pointed out. I hadn't actually thought about that. Maybe Jackson had, and that was why he offered to go.

"What is the actual time?" Mike asked in all seriousness. "Will the shop be open? It was about forty miles away after all."

"Good point. It is five to nine. Should be fine." Kyle replied.

"Hold up. Five to nine?" I found it utterly unfathomable that it was only five to nine. I had lost all concept of time. I had no awareness of the time of day at all.

"I haven't thought about time at all since we arrived. What a thud back into reality." Mum agreed. "I told you we hadn't packed enough, Graham."

"I know, dear."

"Right, I'm off. I'll see you all soon." Jackson saluted as he headed for the door.

"Do you want to be chummed?" I asked, secretly hoping he said no.

"No, that's ok." He kissed my head and left. Thank goodness.

Since it was so early, we'd decided to reconvene in an hour and a half once Jackson had returned and we'd sobered up and processed the early evening's events. I was still living in the buzz of winning the competition, but I couldn't appear to be too happy as that would come across as disrespectful to mum. Even though I knew she was going to be ok. She didn't. What a pickle. What a quandary. I make myself chuckle.

We all head downstairs back to play some games except Claire and mum. Mum goes upstairs to bathe Rubeus. She's had all day to do that, I don't know why she's doing it now, and Claire appears to be a bit more disturbed by what mum said, so I think she just needs a little time to herself to compute and process. Bless her.

Claire

"Do you want to come down and play some games?" Mike asked, holding my hand and noticing I wasn't ready to speak. I shook my head, and he didn't push me. He could see I was upset and just kissed me before leaving with everyone else. I guess he's learned when I need my own space.

I wasn't ready to go downstairs and play happy families. I don't know how everyone else was able to do so. My mum, our mum, is seriously ill. She has cancer. That's not something that should be brushed under the carpet and forgotten about. That's something that needs to be discussed and processed, and I cannot comprehend how my family have been so cold as to move on from such a bombshell so quickly.

I walk through to the kitchen to get myself a glass of water. I've had at least a bottle of wine to myself, and that will not help me compute information. Quite the contrary, really. What if this is the last time we have a family trip with mum? My heart pounds, and my body shakes at the thought. My mum is my best friend. She's the strongest, most giving person I know, and she deserves so much more than her fifty-nine years in this life. I wish there were something I could do to help. I wish I could take her pain.

I walk upstairs. Perhaps, as a selfish act, I wonder if spending solo time with my mum might make me feel better about her situation. I reach the top of the stairs and stand in her bedroom doorway. The upstairs lounge light is off, so she can't see me. I can hear the bath water running for Rubeus. She's humming to herself as she removes her long-sleeved top, probably to avoid the sleeves getting wet and takes Rubeus's collar off.

"Who's a perfect little doggy?" She asks, walking through to the bathroom.

That dog. She is obsessed. She's funny. She doesn't appear to be scared or in pain, nor have I noticed if she has lost any of her hair. I'm so proud of her. I stare into the room, listening to her sing to Rubeus while she bathes him.

"You are my sunshine. My only sunshine. You make me happy when skies are grey. You'll never know, dear, how much I love you. So please don't take my sunshine away."

Mum would sing that to us when we were children. To help us get to sleep, or if we were poorly and sometimes, we'd get a card or a text with nothing in it but those words. It was her song for us. Her children. I guess Rubeus was my new baby brother. Listening to her sing had calmed me, actually. It may be selfish, but I did feel more level-headed now. I went downstairs and walked out onto the porch. It was chilly, but I liked it. It was soothing.

The fog had almost wholly encompassed the lodge. I think if the lodge had been empty and the heating wasn't on, it would be hidden in a thick quilt of mist. There was a distant tingle of precipitation which felt almost dewy as I leant over the porch, attempting to see the garden or the loch. I could barely even see the cars. I don't know how Jackson managed to drive in this. The night felt incredibly still. The lodge was an excellently soundproofed structure as I, surprisingly, couldn't hear a thing coming out of it, and knowing my family like I do, I could only imagine the cacophony that was happening in the games room just now.

I sat down in the corner of the porch and took a deep breath in. It was almost meditative to be out here in the brisk weather, contemplating life and its challenges. I suddenly realised just how selfish I'd been. I had lost a baby and forced the family to mourn with me when my poor mum and dad were facing something much worse. Again, I felt a wave of nausea pull me under like the power of the tide would. My only consolation now is that I appear to be as over my loss as I ever will be. I seem to be out of my negative funk. I appear to be better. One day at a time, if you will. Jesus, Claire. It is so easy to get wrapped up in your own world that you forget how much others are going through. How much people who are close to you may be going through. How little you know about people's personal lives.

I'm reminded of a seminar my work made me go to about being a respectful colleague. We were told how everyone goes through challenges daily, and each challenge brings with it the opportunity for the individual to go into a box. This box is their own world where they are affected by the challenge, negatively or positively, but they are unable to see outside of the box and how their affected moods may be having an effect on those around them. This is precisely what I have been going through for the past three months. I was in my box. I was negatively impacting my loved one's moods because I had tunnel vision. Now that I am out of the box, I can see clearly and have hindsight.

I close my eyes to clear my mind. I can't help what I did and what I put my family through. Everyone deals with grief differently, and unfortunately, I dealt with mine the way I did. We can only move forward from here. I am self-aware again. I start to think about my painting. I paint with my mind. I use wild brushstrokes through my imagination, and I begin to smile. I don't feel as cold as I did when I first came outside. I feel at one with the world. I have some form of inner peace.

Still, with my eyes closed, I sit in harmony with myself. I can hear nothing. If I open my eyes, I can see the sporadic switched on lights of the house reflecting shallowly into the dewy haze. I take another tranquil deep breath and audibly breathe a sigh. Just then, I hear a crack. Like a twig snap? Or a floor creak? Or a window tap? I look around and see nothing. Mainly due to the fog. That was rather spooky. I get shivers as the adrenaline of the fright filters through my body. After a tense moment, I relax back into my previous meditative state.

Crack. Again. What was that? Now I'm scared. Scuff. What was that? Scuff. Scuff. Scuff.

"Hello?" I shakily call out.

The scuff sounds stop. I slowly get up, trying not to make a sound. Is someone there? Is it Jackson?

"Jackson?" I try and sound like I'm not freaked out.

I can feel the hairs on my neck standing taller than ever before. Scuff. There it is again. It's almost like something is dragging on the grass. If it were Jackson, he would have said something sensing that I might be scared. Surely. He has common sense. That means it's not Jackson. That means that something is there. Less than metres away. I cannot see a thing. I am slowly moving towards the door, running my hands along the wall as I do so. Scuff. Again. My heart is in my throat. I don't think I've breathed in minutes. I reach the door, still scanning the area for any sign of life or what the noise might be. I feel the door handle in my hand.

I quickly pull the handle, swing the door open and leap inside. I slam it shut and lock it. I put the chain on and run into Kyle and Steven's room. I make sure their patio doors are locked and stare out onto the porch. Nothing. I don't see anything. There is nothing there. What did I think was there? Now that I feel a bit safer inside and can hear the muffled party happening downstairs, I start to think it might have been an animal. We are in the Scottish glens. It could have been a fox. A wild cat. A deer, even. That would explain the lack of response and scuff on the grass. Perhaps they wouldn't have been able to see me or the lodge and would have just been drawn to the warmth. Yes. Claire. That's rational thinking. I pull myself together and walk around the house, making sure every single window and door is locked, just in case.

Kyle

"Is Claire ok?" I ask Mike as I place the snooker balls into the triangle on the table.

"I think she just needs a little time to process what your mum just told us."

I understand entirely. Claire, like mum, has definitely taken on the worrier role in the family. But, on the other hand, I take everything people tell me at face value. Mum said she is ok and wants to forget about it for the time being; therefore, I feel like we should respect her words and wishes. I am still worried, of course.

"Dad. Level with us. Is mum ok?" I ask, keeping the conversation open and fluid.

"Your mum is my hero. Your mum is positive and has faced her illness with confidence and determination. Just the way she faces every challenge life throws at her."

"Motivational speaker, Graham strikes again!" Steven jokes.

Dad loves to talk in riddles and rhymes and in a way that lays no blame. However, it used to infuriate me. If I asked him a leading question or a question, there could be only one answer to; he would always respond with an elaborate conundrum which would force me to work for the answer. I suppose he was making us problem solvers in his head, but his enigmatic speech would, and still does on many an occasion, exasperate me.

"Right. Well, I'll take that to mean that we carry on as though nothing has happened until mum learns the outcome of her results. If they are negative, we move forward and make adjustments accordingly. If they are positive, then we have a party to celebrate mum. Capiche?"

"I wholeheartedly agree." Ellie said as she wrapped her arms around me. "I believe mum is going to be just fine. I feel it in my fingers."

"Ah, but do you feel it in your toes?" Dad jokes.

Everyone else says yes and nods in agreement. I've always felt like I've had to take the leader role in the family as mum, dad, and Claire are so laid back they are basically lying down. I trained in dance as a child, and now that I'm a manager at work, I have always had to be disciplined and orderly. It feels natural, to be honest, and luckily everyone responds well when I do take charge. I also think it helps that I am virtually always in a positive mood; therefore, when I appear to be on the verge of grumpy, it makes people stand up and notice.

"Come and get beat by me." Ellie drags me over to the TV and turns on Mario kart. Luckily we like this game as it appears to be the only one available.

Dad is playing pool with Mike while Steven, Ellie and I race when mum appears at the door presenting Rubeus like a trophy.

"Isn't he beautiful?" She asks the room.

"But of course." I instantly reply with a hint of sarcasm before dad French kisses him. That is disgusting. I have never understood why dog owners allow their dogs to slobber all over their faces. It is just allowing their dogs to spit all their germs onto their owners. Not to mention the fact that they lick their own bums as well as other dogs' bums.

Once the outrageous display of affection for the dog is complete, mum comes and joins us on the sofa and opts to drive as Luigi.

"I've always had a soft spot for men with a moustache."

"Great to know, mum." I laugh. "Why has dad never had one then?"

"He sometimes does. He always grows one for Valentine's Day." Mum giggled after she finished her sentence as though she was remembering something naughty.

"Alright, mum, less sexual nostalgia, more racing, please!" I could feel Steven and Ellie holding in their laughter, and we all let it out simultaneously.

Claire joined a little while later, and she looked like she'd seen a ghost. She had gone completely white, and she appeared a little shaken up. I know she's a worrier, but she's taking this news a little bit too dramatically.

"Oh Claire, baby, please don't be upset. I'm so sorry I shouldn't have told you." Mum rushed over to her apologetically.

"Oh, no, no. I just had a little scare. That's all. I was outside, and I heard something, and I got a fright. That's all."

Claire seemed seriously out of it.

"What happened, Clairy Fairy?" I asked, now a little worried about her.

"I was just sitting outside enjoying the peace, and I heard an animal or something, that's all. That's all. I couldn't see it because of the fog, and I freaked myself out. That's all. I'm fine. Don't worry, guys."

She was definitely not fine. Mike grabbed her some chocolate, sat her down and wrapped her in a blanket while we all looked at each other and back to Claire. I hugged her, and she was freezing. Poor little lamb. I can't help but think she's being ever so dramatic. I can see Ellie feels the same way, and we give each other an eye roll above Claire's head which prompts Steven to tap me disappointingly. As if he doesn't agree with us too. Goody two shoes.

"It is getting a bit cold. Kyle baby, won't you run up and bring mum her cosy shawl?" Mum asks, referring to herself in the third person.

"Oh sure, it has to be me." I sulk. "What does it look like?"

"It's hanging on the back of the dressing table chair. It's long and black and has a furry bit at the top."

My immature mind makes me giggle at the phallic innuendo in mum's description, which no one else seems to have heard. Normally dad would have. Maybe now is not the time. I leave and run up the stairs. I pop the heating back on since everyone is getting cold. I'm not. But everyone else is. We just can't allow ourselves to be spooked by the pipes again. I check the clock in the kitchen. It is nearly ten. Jackson will be on his way back by now with an overabundance of alcohol which will lift us all back into the party spirit.

I walk upstairs, guided by the light emitting from mum and dad's room. I don't bother to put the upstairs lounge lights on; I just head straight into mum's room. It is madness that I can't hear a thing up here. There's music and talking going on downstairs in the games room, and I wouldn't even be aware of any other presence in the house if I didn't know there was. I scan the room for the shawl, and a shadow throws me in my peripheral vision. I definitely thought I saw someone in the lounge. Obviously, I did not. Everyone is downstairs. Christ. Claire has put the fear in me.

I scan the room again in the dead silence and spot the elusive chair and shawl; both sat surreptitiously propping open a wardrobe door. I go to grab the shawl and notice something strange in the open wardrobe. There's a light coming from inside, and as I get nearer, I see the light is coming from the back of it, where it appears to be broken. I look even closer. It is a door. A door? I push it ever so slightly. It opens to a rickety looking landing and an even more unstable staircase, lit only by a very dim bulb overhead. There is a bolt latch on the door's hidden side, which means it can only be locked from inside. My heart starts to race. What is this? Why is it here? Why is it hidden by a wardrobe? Where does it lead? I hear something like footsteps coming from behind me. I scurry back and out of the wardrobe. I turn around with my heart thumping in my chest. What -.

All

"Kyle is taking his time." Steven commented with a raised eyebrow.

He had been a while, but he was probably just making mum wait for her shawl since she made him go to get it.

"Go and get him, Ellie?" Mum commanded with a condescending tone.

Of course, she would ask me to go. Never Claire. I was in the middle of a race.

"It's ok. I'll run up and get him." Steven says.

Thank goodness. He's probably on the toilet. I chuckle to myself. At that moment, everything goes dark. The TV shuts off, the lights go out, and my heart skips a beat with fright.

"What just happened?" I ask the room.

"I think we've just had another power cut." Dad says rather calmly.

"Another power cut?" I ask, somewhat alarmed.

"We had one in the middle of the night last night, but your mum and I sorted it. Follow the sound of my voice, and everyone link hands."

I wish Jackson were here.

I held mum's hand at the front and Claire's hand at the back. I think mum had Steven's hand, who had dad's, and Mike was at the back behind Claire. This was not enjoyable. We made our way up the stairs with fewer trips than I expected. When we reached the top, mum and dad broke away and told us to go upstairs, and Steven broke away to go and find Kyle. I think we were planning on retiring somewhere comfy for the final portion of the evening. That meant I had to lead the way. I ran my hand along the edge of the staircase and found the bottom of the stairs.

"Kyle?" I called.

No answer.

"Babe, you're not funny. There's been a power cut." Steven shouted, sounding rather cross.

"I've never heard either of you be grumpy with each other." I whispered as an observation.

"That's because we both know when enough is enough, and right now, it's over the line."

Steven was definitely cross. He went into their bedroom to check if Kyle was in there while we staggered up the stairs with more stumbles than before. These stairs were definitely more significant than those leading to the basement. Finally, we reached the top and let go of each other's hands. I knew exactly where the big sofa was and jumped onto it. Might as well get comfy. I wish Jackson were here.

-

I had a tight grip on Graham's hand, and I could feel our palms getting clammy. I didn't care to be honest. It had been quite an eventful evening. I needed a stiff drink upon Jackson's return. It appeared we were heading the right way, but we tripped up on something. A bit of rope by the feel of it. I don't remember there being any rope in the dining area. One of the kids must have had it for some reason. We get up and continue our blind expedition. Just as we started to move forward again, we stopped as we heard a noise. Was that a door opening? Or closing?

"Kyle?" Graham asked, sounding hopeful.

Silence.

"Kyle, if that's you, don't be silly. There's been a power cut, and we can't see anything." Graham wasn't happy.

"Kyle wouldn't do that, Graham." I know he wouldn't. He's not a practical joker. That didn't explain what we heard, though. It was probably one of the others heading upstairs.

"It doesn't help that the fog is preventing moonlight from shining in through the windows."

"I know. Once we get to the fuse box, it'll be fine."

"This needs to be mentioned in the review."

"Of course, dear."

We reach the cupboard where the fuse box is kept. Within seconds, Graham has the power back on, but he doesn't look as happy this time.

"That wasn't normal."

"What do you mean?" What does he mean?

"Well, usually you just need to flick this button as sometimes, if too much power is being used for the capability of the building, it switches off for safety purposes. But this time, the mains power was switched off."

"So someone turned the power off?" I asked, slightly confused.

"Yes." Graham confirmed.

We heard a scream come from upstairs. It must be Kyle frightening them. Little rascal. I didn't think he would do that.

"That's not funny, Kyle." Graham muttered.

-

I let go of Ellie's hand, and I found the light switch along the side of the wall and waited for mum and dad to get the power back up and running so I could turn the lights on. Mike stayed with me and held me, which was very comforting. I was over this evening. I didn't really want whatever Jackson was bringing back. I just wanted to go to bed, to be honest.

"Kyle? You're not funny." Steven was still calling on Kyle as he made his own way up the stairs. I was surprised at him, actually. As much as he is a joker, he knows where the line is.

The light in mum's bedroom flicked on, and I could see the lights from downstairs come back on, so I clicked the dimmer switches in my hand to turn on the lounge lights.

"What the hell?" Ellie shouted, jumping up from the sofa.

"What's wrong?" I asked, slightly annoyed at Ellie for being so obnoxious.

"Babe." Mike said, staring at something with a furrowed brow.

I turned to see what he was staring at, and I let out a scream. I started to shake. I did hear someone outside. Kyle wouldn't do this. This wasn't Kyle. He wouldn't. Someone was outside. Someone has been inside the lodge. Where is Kyle?

"KYLE?" Steven shouted through the lodge before starting to cry. "What the fuck is going on?"

I rush to Steven. "I don't know; I don't know. First, we need to find Kyle; then, I'm sure all will become clear. Maybe it's an elaborate prank."

"It's not a prank. Kyle isn't a prankster." Steven instantaneously responded. I knew he wasn't, but I was trying to keep us both calm. Ellie and Mike hadn't moved since seeing it.

I called on mum and dad, who were halfway up the stairs, in a slight panic, as they were unaware of what was going on.

"What's happening up here?" Mum said as she reached the top of the stairs before stopping dead in her tracks when she saw it.

"KYLE. This is not funny." Dad bellowed as soon as he arrived. Dad never raised his voice. This was serious. He was scared.

"It's not Kyle, Graham. He wouldn't do this." Steven said. He suddenly sprinted through the top floor and then ran downstairs. I presumed he was looking for Kyle.

I moved towards my vandalised painting. The painting I'd worked on this very afternoon. I looked at it and how it was sitting on top of the easel. The easel I had last seen down in the games room. The easel that Mike and dad had struggled to put together. Someone had been in the games room and had taken it all the way up here. How had they managed to do that? I looked closer and saw how whoever had defaced it had grabbed it and had left a fist imprint in the centre where they'd carried it from our bedroom to the easel. I saw how they'd pressed hard against the canvas in order to write their intimidating message on my beautiful picture.

The message read: WE ARE WATCHING YOU.

Who are we? Why are they watching us? I felt sick again. Mainly because I know someone was outside with me. Where is Kyle?

Steven arrived back upstairs out of breath. "I can't find Kyle." He agitatedly looked at us all, holding back tears before turning the lights off. I'd been so engrossed in my defaced painting that I hadn't noticed Steven turning all the lights off down the stairs too.

"Why did you turn the lights off?" Ellie asked, sounding slightly panicked.

"Because someone is watching us." Dad answered for Steven.

"But surely if Kyle is missing and this painting is here, then they must be in the house?" Mike pointed out.

Mum started to sob.

"How is this happening?" Dad asked incredulously. "This isn't real."

All

I can't breathe. I am trying to inhale, but it's like there's no oxygen around me. I fall with tears streaming down my face and use the bannister for support. I can't feel my legs. They are completely numb. I am taking deep guttural gasps of air, trying to regain my breath, but it doesn't seem to be helping. My chest feels tight, which gives the sensation that my heartbeat is getting bigger in alarm. I give up on my legs as my arms grow tired, and I allow my body to slide down the wall next to the bannister in an attempt to calm myself. I close my eyes and concentrate on nothing. I open my eyes and look at Graham. I am having a panic attack. I breathe in through my nose and out through my mouth. I will catch my breath. I squeeze my toes and my calves, and my thighs. Again. Again. Graham helps me to my feet, and I weekly lean on the wall while focussing on ensuring my circulation is normal. Rubeus is there by my ankles. He's always by my side. I can stand on my own two feet, breathe regularly, and wipe the tears from my eyes and take control.

"No one leaves this room." I say as no one had spoken in what felt like a long time.

"We will figure this out." I continue moving towards the centre of the lounge and sitting on the coffee table. "Ellie, you will go and get mine and your dad's phones. Mike, go and get you and Claire's. Steven, your car is at the back of the drive. Where are your car keys?"

"They're in our room, somewhere." Steven stuttered.

Graham put his hand around my shoulders and gave me a light squeeze. I knew he was willing me to continue, but I was going to slowly run out of ideas.

Mike returned with their phones, both of which had zero signal and the same with Graham and I's. So I gave one to each couple or half of them. Just in case there was a moment of service.

"Should we go and get the car keys and our phones?" Ellie asked, referring to herself and Steven.

"I don't know how safe that sounds." Graham warned.

Mike threw Steven an ornament that looked hardily solid, and Ellie picked up a vase.

"We'll be quick, dad."

"Be back in five minutes, and don't turn any lights on. I don't care if you don't have the phones. Just get back here with the car keys in five minutes." I ordered, and Steven set his watch on a timer.

Mike, Claire, Graham and I sit on the edge of the coffee table as they leave. There is something about sitting on the wooden coffee table that makes me feel more on edge than if we were to stand or sit on a sofa. More ready to jump up and run. More prepared for action.

-

I feel like my heartbeat is making a lot of noise as Steven and I slink down the stairs, decorative weapons held high. Steven is leading the way, and as we reach the bottom of the stairs, he slowly enters his bedroom.

"I didn't see anyone when I was looking for Kyle." He whispered. I don't know how to respond. Where the hell was Kyle? My brother and my best friend was missing, and it appeared as though our family holiday was being hijacked by some sick, sadistic creep. I stood in the doorway with my vase raised aloft, ready to smack it onto anyone that came in. I could see out both the lounge windows and the patio doors in the boys' bedroom from where I was standing. The fog is still dense. I can barely see metres past the porch. That stunning view is hidden. How had Jackson managed to drive in that? Why had we not thought about the fog when he volunteered to leave? Why had I not been more forceful in going with him? Where was he? What time was it? He'd be back soon, surely? If he was here, I'd feel much calmer. I miss him. At least I know where he is. Steven must be dying inside.

"Got the keys. But I can't find our phones. I'm sure Kyle put his in his bedside drawer, but it's not there, and I was sure mine was in my jacket pocket, but it's not there." Steven whispered, slightly panicked.

"Ok, we'll go get ours." I said as I strode out confidently and walked around the corner towards the stairs that led downstairs. What was I doing? My heart got stronger with every step I took towards the stairs, as though my body was telling me to stop. Which I did as I reached the top. Steven, in the dark, obviously hadn't seen me stop as he bumped into the back of me before cuddling me from behind.

"We don't have to go down." He assured me. "If Kyle and I's phones are not there, there's also the chance that your phone is missing too."

I couldn't speak. I was furious with myself. Why was I not being brave? My family were in trouble, and I was doing nothing to help.

"You've chummed me to get the car keys. That's the most important thing, Ellie." Steven continued after my silence. "Let's just go back upstairs. We don't have enough time left anyway."

Now I thought it wasn't just me who was scared to go downstairs. Steven was apprehensive, too, so I gave him a nod, he took my hand, and we headed to go back up the stairs.

-

What did it mean by; we are watching you? Have they been watching since we arrived? Is that what the design of the house is for? To be easily viewed from all angles. Is it the lodge owners who have made this house and have people come to it on holiday and then torture them? Has this happened before? Surely it would have been in the news. This feels personal. Why would they write over my painting? They knew I painted. Did they watch me paint? They would have watched me have sex. Is it they? They said we. We are watching you. Not I. We. There is more than one person involved in this sick orchestration.

Mike grabbed my hand and gave it a squeeze. I wanted to be close to him in order to feel safe, but I didn't want to reach a feeling of comfort and not be ready for action. I looked at mum, and her eyes were fixed on the top of the staircase. Dad's too. Mike could sense my discomfort at his hand on mine and instead gave me a lasting kiss on my head and stood up. I hadn't noticed, but I have been flicking my focus from the two doorways in the room to the outside consistently. Just to be aware and alert, I guess.

"What's the plan, mum?" I asked in a hushed tone.

Mum didn't respond.

I looked at the phone that mum had given me. It was half past ten. Jackson would be due back soon.

I looked outside. It looked as though the fog was thinning. Was that just my imagination? At least we couldn't be seen anymore. But, I suppose that didn't matter if those watching us had come into the lodge. I shuddered at the thought. Someone has actually been inside the lodge while we were unaware and plotted to frighten us. Possibly schemed to hurt us and has perhaps already hurt Kyle. This is a nightmare. Never has that saying been more apt. I am terrified and confused. This is a nightmare.

A creak comes from downstairs. It sounded like a step. I know it should be Ellie and Steven, but what if it isn't? What if they've been hurt or gone missing too? What if they're still downstairs, and those who are watching us have snuck by them. The first thing I see coming up the stairs is a big gold vase, the vase that Ellie had taken for protection. I breathe a slight sigh of relief, and as I lock eyes with Ellie, they both hurry up the rest of the stairs and over to us.

"I got the car keys, but our phones have gone missing." Steven informed us, perching on the arm of the sofa and looking to mum for the next step of her plan. I think she has a plan. So does Steven, by the looks of things. Kyle always has a plan. He'd take control just now.

-

There are six of us, and I hadn't thought it through completely yet.

"We are going to make our way down to Steven's car, and we are going to drive to go and get help." I announce to the group, still keeping my voice low.

"But there's six of us, mum. Plus Rubeus." Claire interjected.

"We will squeeze in." I assured.

"But what about Kyle?" Steven asked. "I can't leave without him."

"We don't know where he is right now. I know he is ok, but we cannot help him by sitting idly and waiting for him to turn up. We have to go and get help." I felt my voice shaking as I spoke, and my eyes filled with tears as I stopped talking. I couldn't believe what I was saying or what I was leading my family through. I looked around, and everyone seemed to have their attention on me.

"When we get to the car, Steven, if you drive, Graham will get in the passenger seat, and the rest of us will jump in the back. Reverse the car as fast as you can down the road. Hopefully, we'll pass Jackson on the way."

I have never been more scared in all my life.

-

Mike pulled my arm as if I had been in a daze, and we all appeared to be on the move. Where were we going? Come on, Claire. Pull yourself together.

As we walked down the stairs, we lent on the wall and slid ourselves down, placing as little weight as possible on the stairs to avoid making noise. Aside from the hush of our clothes grazing the wall, the lodge was silent. I couldn't hear a thing. Dead silence. That in itself was more frightening than if we could hear anything. If there is silence, then they, whoever they are, must be watching. Can they see us trying to escape? Are there cameras in the house?

We reach the door, and mum peels back the chain latch before slowly turning the locks on the doors.

"When I open the door, run." She whispers to us.

In a split second, mum has swung the door open, and we are hit with the cold air as we leap out of the lodge, off the porch and through the fog to reach the cars. What if we bump into someone in the fog? I'd heard someone earlier this evening. I want to scream at the thought, but I keep quiet, finding Mike and I's car. I can see Steven's. He's already there. All the doors are open. Mum and Rubeus are in; Mike is in, I'm in, dad is in, Ellie is in; the doors are shut and locked.

-

"Hurry up, Steven!" I start to panic as I lay over Mike and Claire.

The ignition was turning, but the car wasn't starting.

"The car won't start." Steven shrieked.

"Stay calm." Dad said. "Push the accelerator down and turn the key."

"I am. We put the car in for a service last week. This isn't normal, Graham."

I can't believe what I'm hearing. I look out of the windows in a bid to see anything, and as I scan round to the front of the car, I spot something. A post-it note on the air freshener hanging from the rearview mirror.

"What's this?" I ask, leaning in and grabbing it. "You can't leave."

"What?" Claire asks, taking the note from me. "Are you fucking kidding me?"

"What? What is it?" Dad asked, sounding shocked as Claire never swears.

"It's a note that says; you can't leave." I say and hand it to dad.

"The car isn't starting, guys." Steven gives in.

"Let me try ours." Mike says, jumping out of the car. We watch him run over and jump in. Ten or twenty seconds go by before we see him turn around and shake his head.

"These sadistic bastards." Dad snarled.

We are trapped. I look out the window and stare back at the lodge as we all sit in silence, probably in an attempt to form some sort of plan.

"We could walk down the road and hope that Jackson comes back and takes us to get help?" I offer.

"But what if 'they' are waiting down the road for us?" Claire asks.

"I don't know." I start to cry. Again, I look out of the window and stare back at the lodge. Wait. "I can see the lodge."

"The fog must be clearing." Dad says. "Or moving."

"Is that a good thing or a bad thing?" Steven asks.

Pass. No one answers.

-

"Mum? What do you think we should do?" I ask, hoping she has a better idea than what I was about to suggest. But instead of answering, she just looks at me with tears in her eyes.

Right. "We should go back inside and figure out a plan. Lock ourselves in one of the rooms and wait for Jackson or for signal." I think I spoke with conviction. What if I'm making a mistake? What if this is the wrong decision?

"Are you sure?" Steven asks.

"Yes. Let's go to mum and dad's room." Why do I sound so confident when I'm screaming inside?

I open the car door spontaneously and make my way to the porch, hoping that everyone is following me. I reach the door, which is still ajar and push through, turning around to close it once everyone is in. I slam the door shut, lock it and put the chain latch on before following the group up the stairs. Steven and Mike close and lock the door behind me, barricading it with the bed for an extra measure.

All

I was frozen. I had sat down in one of the chesterfield chairs in the corner of the room with Rubeus in my arms, and I couldn't move. This was surreal. There are people actively trying to scare and hurt my family and me. Why are they doing this? Is it a game, or do they know who we are? Is it random or personal? There was so much I wanted to discuss with my family, to try and figure a way to safety, but I was frozen. Not just my body. My mouth. I looked around, and everyone seemed to be in the same situation. My mind had so many questions and was still in a flutter of panic that it was working overload, and my body couldn't take energy away from it to move.

Claire knelt down by me and draped her body over my legs. As though the contact broke me free, I took a sharp intake of breath. Had I not breathed since I sat down? Surely I had. The room looked at me in fright at my audible inhale, and I gesticulated to show I was alright; it was just a tic.

Now that I was consistently breathing again, my mind slowly started to clear, and I began pinpointing moments that seemed eerily suspicious from throughout the weekend. Right from the very beginning, I was left slightly befuddled when I tipped back the plant pot to reveal only one key.

"The owner had assured me both over the phone and via email that two keys would be left for us upon arrival." I spoke out of the blue. "I never thought much of it, condemning it as human error. Now I'm not so sure. There was only one key left on the porch." I seem to have everyone's fixed attention. "What if these people have the other key?" There is silence. "They have full access to the house."

"That means that this was definitely planned." Ellie whispered, turning away and fighting back the tears.

"Of course, it was planned, Ellie." Claire snapped.

"We will not snap or turn on each other. Claire. This situation is incomparable, and we will all deal with it differently but let's not take it out on each other." The control I appeared to possess previously has returned. "There have been two power cuts throughout this weekend. Now, I put that down to us being ignorant of our energy consumption; however, I am definitely sure they were deliberate attacks, or scares, or stages in this sadistic event."

"I agree." Graham said. "Someone had just turned off the mains switch the second time."

"But why? There must be a reason for them to do that." Mike offered.

"I have no idea, unfortunately." I genuinely didn't. "We don't know how well these people know this lodge. It's huge. When your dad and I went to fix the electricity the second time, we tripped up on a knot of rope. Was that any of yours?"

"No. Definitely not. Why would we have rope? Oh god."

"Stay calm, Claire." Mike reminded her.

-

"Stay calm?" Why would someone ask me to do that when we are being hunted like animals? "Well, might I remind everyone that we heard the person who switched off the electric and brought rope into the house?"

"When?" Ellie asked jarringly.

"When we were playing dominoes." Steven realised. "But Jackson and I went to look. He didn't see anything, and I didn't hear anything." He continued, almost defensively.

"But like mum said, we don't know how well they know this house. They might have been looking at the lodge from out there, outside, where they might have spotted hideaways in living areas that we would never touch. This is a massive building, and they have observed it from two aspects."

"Why are you so sure they have been watching us from outside?" Ellie pried again.

"Because when I was sitting outside, I heard them. I heard them trying to scare me or trying to reach the lodge without hurting themselves through the fog. I don't know. But I do know that they were there, metres away from me on the porch. I thought it was an animal. I hoped it was an animal." I shuddered, recalling. Furthermore, how else would they know I painted? I was sitting at the window all day, and I never saw anyone aside from the boys fishing. There was no one in the house but Ellie. We would have realised if someone else was in the building; surely."

"Claire..." Mike whispered. "Oh god, I feel sick."

"What?" I didn't have patience for dramatics.

"Claire." Mike looked at me with tears in his eyes and grabbed me. In his embrace, he whispered in my ear. "When you were in the shower."

My stomach twisted into a knot, and I wretched.

"What is it?" Mum seemed slightly unnerved and agitated at Mike and I's behaviour, and her annoyance forced Rubeus to jump out of her arms.

"Yesterday." Oh god, I had to relive it again. "When I went for a shower." I was struggling to say it out loud, knowing that it wasn't Mike or one of the boys. "When I was in the shower. Someone, who I thought at the time was Mike, came into the bathroom. They didn't say anything, but they moved close to the shower. I spoke to them as though they were Mike, and then they left." I shivered as I finished recounting the horrific memory, and Mike punched the bed in frustration.

-

"So someone. One of these 'watchers' was in the bathroom while you were showering?" I asked, trying to process all this information.

"Yes, Ellie." Mum confirmed as Claire was still shuddering to herself.

I was seriously struggling to fathom all of this. When I napped earlier on when Jackson was on his run, did I dream he came back or was someone in the room? Had they been so blazon as to go into a room that we were in? If they did it to Claire, then I saw no reason why they wouldn't be so confident as to come into my room while I was sleeping.

"I think someone came into my bedroom while I was napping earlier on. I stirred and thought it was Jackson, but when I woke up, later on, he said he was just back." I told the group rather calmly.

"These people must be mentally corrupt." Steven was disgusted at what I'd said.

"What's more, Kyle and I tried to get into the boiler room downstairs yesterday. I picked the lock, and we managed to open it, but something was inside which prevented us from opening the door any more than a slither."

"Something, or someone?" Claire asked.

"Well." I continued.

"Oh god." Mum whimpered.

"At the time, we thought it was the boiler making some sort of noise, but now, in hindsight, I think it might have actually been a person breathing in there."

"Are you serious?" Steven asked. "Is that what you two were doing when I came down to get you?"

I nodded. Where was Jackson? I looked out of the window to see if there was any sign of his imminent return.

"If we catch Jackson's car coming up the drive, we could maybe run and jump into it. At least we know his car will be working." I say, relatively happy with my plan.

"Good idea, Elle." Dad said, stroking my back.

I wish Jackson was here now. He'd help me make sense of what is happening. Jackson, or a shower. Although, I don't see myself enjoying a shower for a long time after hearing what happened to Claire.

"This is so fucked up. We should have been suspicious as soon as we arrived. We are literally being watched twenty-four-seven because the windows provide a cinema viewing screen, with no curtains, into our lives."

I could sense how frustrated Mike was as he spat his words.

I completely agree. That was the first thing I picked up on. At least downstairs, the windows were shallow and were only at the tops of the walls, but there were no walls up here, only floor to ceiling windows.

I returned to staring out of one of the windows in the hope of catching the glare of Jackson's car lights piercing through the fog. He probably had to drive slowly to be safe through the mist, and at least we knew he was safe, which is more than we knew about Kyle's whereabouts.

"I bet it was them. They smashed the boat." Dad said out of the blue.

Both Steven and Mike agreed.

"What happened to the boat?" Claire asked. "I noticed you sat on the bank rather than get in the boat."

"The bottom of the boat had been smashed, and it sank." Dad informed us all.

"But why?" Mike asked.

"They told us in the note they left in Steven and Kyle's car. We can't leave. They're removing all our escape routes."

"Shelly, do you think what we saw today is where these people have been staying?" Steven asks. "If so, is that why Rubeus went nuts over the sleeping bag?"

"What did you find today?" I ask hastily.

"We came across a small clearing while we were out walking." Steven said.

"We thought it looked like an old campsite. There was an old sleeping bag that Rubeus was tearing apart, small dips where bodies had laid, a small black campfire in the centre and some rubbish that had been left there."

"What colour was the sleeping bag?" I asked, remembering that I'd found two sleeping bags in the cupboard downstairs along with three of everything else.

"Seriously, Ellie? That's what you took from that story?" Claire jibed.

"It was blue. Why?" Mum answered and asked.

"Yes, Claire. I found a rucksack of camping stuff downstairs, and there were three of everything except sleeping bags. There were only two sleeping bags, and they were blue."

"Where did you find this?" Claire was now interested in what I had to say.

"In the locked cupboard in the games room."

"You don't think that whoever these people are camped out nearby until they could steal the key to move in?" Claire theorised.

"Maybe they're squatters who are just playing a game with us." Steven continued.

"But where are they? Why can't we see them, and where have they been while we have been here? I know the lodge is big, but surely one of us would have come across three people squatting at some point over the weekend?" Mum shook her head. "This is premeditated."

"They knew where to find the key. They knew what we were doing. They knew when we were doing it. They know things about the lodge that we don't. They know their way around the area. They knew we'd use the boat. They knew we'd try and drive away. They are sick sadistic people, and they are here to hurt us." Dad evidently agreed with mum.

"We can't forget that Kyle is missing. Something happened to him within ten minutes of him leaving to get Shell's shawl and the power cut."

"We know, Steven, baby." Mum sighed. "These people have our Kyle somewhere. Possibly hurt."

"Possibly dead." Steven sobbed, and Mike wrapped his arm around him, which made mum cry too.

"We can't say that. We don't know anything for sure." Mum said through tears.

I get comfy kneeling on the dressing table while staring into the thinning fog, praying to the god I don't believe in that I'll spot Jackson's car coming soon. I listen to Steven and mum sob while Rubeus whimpers at his mum to cheer up, and Claire lets out the odd angry huff. I'm just like dad. We look to those around us for help and support in times of trouble. I'm definitely a follower, not a leader. Please, Jackson, come back for us.

Shelley

I sit still and I wait for an answer to come. I hope and I pray that it is all a joke and that my husband and babies are safe. I am crying because I am scared, and I am confused, and I am panicked because this situation is surreal; how can one navigate themselves through such an event? I am angry at the fact that some people can be this cruel, and I am sad because we don't know what is to come, we don't know where Kyle is, and we still have no plan for escape. We have been in this room for what feels like hours, but when I look at my watch, I'm shocked to see it's only just eleven o'clock. Jackson should definitely be due back any minute now. The roads must be in bad condition for him to drive so slowly.

Furthermore, we have been in darkness for about an hour now; I wonder if 'they' can still see us or if they are preoccupied with Kyle, wherever they have my baby boy. If they are still watching, they must be getting bored since we aren't providing any entertainment right now.

Bored, or getting ready to strike; prepared to claim their next prize, ready to continue their attack.

The silence is deafening in here. No one is crying, rocking, shivering, or frustrated anymore; instead, I think everyone has internalised what has happened and is starting to plan ahead. That's an emotional place where I need to be. I just can't stop thinking about these horrid people and why they are doing this. Rubeus notices when I stir from my daydream and bounces over to me. I pick him up, and he nuzzles into my chest. My little man. Although he is acting slightly torpidly, he doesn't understand what's going on, and I'm so thankful for his ignorant and unconditional love right now.

I look up and watch my family. My practical and industrious family who are refusing to become victims in life. They look as though they are preparing for battle as they utilise their resourcefulness to full effect.

Ellie is fashioning a Rapunzel-like rope with the bedding; I can only imagine that can be for if we need to escape from up here. How would I get Rubeus down? I shake my head. This only happens in films. Graham has taken the legs off of his chair to use as a sort of bat, and I have to admit, they look solid and dangerous. Mike takes the large ornaments from around the room, putting them into pillow cases and tying the tops. Steven has thought the opposite way, and instead of thinking attack and escape, he has focussed on defence. He has barricaded both; the door in a more secure manner and the windows as best he can. He has jarred the door shut with slats from the bed and made sure the door can't open further by placing the dresser in front of it. He has also used all the remaining furniture to block the windows in a bid to prevent anyone from seeing into this room.

As the creativity resolves, everyone settles in a coiled position.

"Do we think there's three of them, then?" Steven asked, breaking the silence, which surprised us as no one responded.

"If it was their stuff I found downstairs, most likely." Ellie replied after a moment.

"Plus, there were definitely three indents where people had slept in the camp in the wood." I added with a crack in my voice. I was thirsty. I got up and went to get some water from the en-suite.

"So...do we think that...they know that we know...how many there are?" Steven asked, slightly confusing himself as he spoke.

"Yes. Why else would they write 'We' on my painting?" Claire impatiently snapped.

"Good point. Absolutely." Steven panders to Claire's mood. "But what I mean is...do they hope that we think there are more than three? Do they want us to feel like there's some sort of ring of them surrounding us?" Steven reiterated, trying to be eloquent.

"I think three is quite a sufficient number to surround an innocent and helpless family." Graham answered for everyone, and his words resonated as they shut the conversation down. "I'm sorry. I think I'm just still in shock. There is no knowing how many of them there are."

"We all are in shock." I walk towards Graham, put my glass down, take his hands in mine, and we dance. We sway and move our feet to the rumba footwork, and we remember what life is about and why it is worth living. After a minute, I open my eyes, and my heart swells. I see Mike with Claire and Ellie with Steven copying us. Dancing. Reminding each other of their reasons for living. Bless them.

I don't want to let go. Before I took Graham to dance, I felt weak, and I was shivering slightly, but I now felt strong, and my teeth had stopped chattering. I can do anything with Graham by my side. We can do anything as a family.

"Is anyone else hungry?" Ellie asks, breaking away from Steven.

"Absolutely starving. I feel like I have a hangover." Claire immediately answered.

I was sure I had a bag of sweeties in my bag somewhere. So I had a rummage but then I remembered Graham and I had eaten them instead of buying a snack at the last petrol station.

"Please tell me you're hunting for food, mum?" Ellie asked, noticing me delving in about my bags.

"I'm sorry, sweetness, I don't have anything."

"Toothpaste?" Mike offers, having already retrieved my whitening Colgate from the en-suite. Mike loved anything mint flavoured, but I don't know how healthy it would be to eat toothpaste, let alone how he was managing to stomach it.

"I'm not sure that's entirely healthy, Mike." Graham said before I had a chance to judge him.

Mike shrugged and continued to eat little bits at a time, and we all seemed to have forgotten our situation for a moment as the atmosphere in the room became a little more relaxed. I even found myself smiling at Mike.

My smile switches quickly to wide-eyed panic as we hear a clunk come from outside. As a group, we rush to grab a weapon from the pile of fashioned munitions made earlier before positioning ourselves strategically along the window, masked with various furniture pieces, including the mattress, for added invisibility. I peer out over the chest of drawers but below the dressing table through the lookout hole with Ellie. The fog is definitely thinning; I can see so much more than I could before; I can even almost make out the shapes of the trees. The clunk sounded wooden, so my first instinct was to try and scan the loch and jetty for evidence or a clue as to what caused the noise. Albeit the fog prevented us from seeing anything more than misty outlines, my eyes caught a slight movement on the patch of grass stretching out from the porch. I focussed on the moving shadow that appeared to be drawing closer to the lodge, and I quickly realised that it was, in fact, a person. I heard Claire take a sharp intake of breath as she spotted the person too. It wasn't Jackson; this person is much too short. They are dressed all in black with a black hoodie which hides the top of their head. This is it. They're going to unlock the door, come up the stairs, get in the room and get us all. I can't tear myself away from my lookout, staring at this figure who is confidently striding through the fog until they stop and begin to scan the lodge. Were they looking for us? Did they not know where we were? As soon as they see the furniture piled up against the window, I presume they'll know we are in here. The figure looks up and straight at our window. They are wearing a balaclava, so we can't see their face. They wave. They know we are in here. Was it a bad idea to barricade ourselves in? Should we have just made a run for it through the fog?

The figure's face moves slightly to the right, stops waving and points to our room. Why is it pointing? Is it pointing to us for someone? Is it telling someone in the house where we are? How does it know for sure we are in here? Can it see us in the dark?

BANG. I let out a sharp scream. There's someone outside the bedroom, in the lounge. It sounded like they just punched the door. Steven goes towards the door and holds a chair leg above his head. Ellie is right behind him with another leg. We remain silent in fear and trepidation. I turn back around to keep my eye on the figure outside, realising that no one is watching them, and they have moved ever so slightly round to the right-hand side. They haven't moved closer. Why have they not moved closer? Is this part of their game? What is happening outside the bedroom? As I finish my last thought, a scratching sound comes from the wall next to the bedroom door. Again, I let out a little squeal, and Rubeus loses his patience by beginning to bark at the door before Graham scoops him up and hushes him.

"What do you want from us?" Steven calls out. Silence. "What the fuck do you want?"

The scratching sound returns, and it seems as though something is being dragged down the wall and down the stairs. I have not averted my gaze from the original figure outside, and I notice they get distracted by something downstairs. Slowly, a new figure joins the original; this one has emerged from the lodge and is carrying a long bat shaped weapon; not dissimilar to our chair legs. This must be the figure who made the noises outside the room. They stand together and stare at our window. Had that figure been in the lodge the whole time? I hadn't heard anyone moving outside of the room. Where had they been hiding? I felt sick.

Having stared at these two figures for so long, my eyes start to blur; I ask Ellie to swap so I can turn back into the room, and I notice everyone is still on edge. Steven has remained motionless at the door with a chair leg, and Mike and Graham are still covering his back.

Rubeus's attention catches mine as I discern he is staring at the cupboard that had caused a fright for us both last night. He was growling lightly but intimidatingly at it, and my heart sank. Please, tell me no one is in there. I stood up and moved towards it slowly, trying to avoid spooking anyone with my panic. My heart was racing as I placed my hand on the knob and pulled the door open slowly. It was empty. Again. I leave the door open to hopefully ease Rubeus's stress, but he stays there, warning the thin air with his rumble.

What on earth was he seeing that none of us could? I sat down next to the cupboard, and as I did, he moved closer to it with me.

"Why are they just standing there?" Ellie asked, still staring out at them.

"Maybe waiting on the third person emerging?" Steven suggested. "If there is a third person."

"Or waiting on an entire crowd of the sadistic fuckers arriving?" Mike offered more aggressively.

"Why is Jackson not back yet?" Ellie whimpered a little.

"Be thankful he isn't back yet, darling." I comforted her from afar. "At least he isn't embroiled in this situation."

"Shell." Graham said my name and pointed to Rubeus.

"I know; he just hates this cupboard; I don't know why."

"No. Shell, look at his head."

I looked at his head, somewhat worried about what Graham was seeing, and then I noticed it too. A thin strip of light that ran across his head was travelling from within the cupboard. I looked inside and saw the line of light coming from the right-hand side of the cupboard. What is that? I can't deal with any more of this.

In a fit of having had quite enough nonsense for one night, I gave the back of the cupboard a push, the sound of which made the group turn and watch me.

"Ellie, keep watching those fuckers." I said without looking back, knowing she'd have turned as well.

The back of the cupboard swung open with a little force revealing something I did not expect. I have discovered a landing and a staircase, lit by a very dim low-hanging bulb overhead. What is this? Where does this lead? It looks as though this staircase has been blocked off altogether - bar the conspicuous entry via the back of a cupboard. No. This is not happening. This is absolutely too surreal to be happening. This lodge will not be the death of me.

"I don't know what is going on, but quite frankly, I don't care anymore." I spit.

"This will be why they're staring at us. They're probably worried we find this hidden room." Claire proposed while inspecting the new find.

"Or they wanted us to find this, and it's a trap." I couldn't see what the use of this hideaway landing was, and I was getting angry.

"I have an idea." Ellie declared. "Why don't we write a message on the window, and when we see Jackson drive up, turn the lights on so he can read it and hopefully, he'll reverse straight away to go and get help?"

"Good idea." Any idea was a good idea at this point. "Grab my make-up bag, Claire." I command. "And do your thing with this door, Steven." I refer to the newfound door and landing, hoping he blockades it as well as he did the main door. "Let's save ourselves with a message on a window."

Kyle

There is grit in my mouth. Why is there grit in my mouth? Is that grit? Or is my mouth so dry it feels like grit? I'm still in a deep sleep state where I can't move my body yet. That's fine; I'll deal with the grit until I feel able to wake up. Which won't be any time soon because I definitely have a hefty hangover. I haven't moved yet, but already my head is throbbing, and my body is sore. I must have drank even more than I would typically allow myself to last night; actually, I'm surprised Steven let me get so drunk. What were we doing?

I remember being in the games room and drinking quite a lot of wine, then we were in the downstairs lounge drinking dad's cocktails. Then we were...back in the games room? Then Jackson went to the shop. That's it. It must have been whatever Jackson brought back for us.

Thinking is making my headache worse, so I focus on the silence in the room. Why is there silence? Why can't I hear Steven's purring? It takes all the strength I have to muster the energy so I can peel one eye open to spy on Steven. I open my eye and see nothing except darkness. Ok, I will have to move now, and I really don't want to. This is going to split my head in two. At least I can get a drink and make my mouth feel better.

I roll my arm round from the side of my body to help push myself up. I don't think I'm on the bed. Have I fallen out of bed? Is that why my body hurts? As I place my palm flat down, I realise I'm on the ground. It is cold, hard concrete. Oh lord, where am I? The floor in the bedroom is wooden, and the rest of the house is wooden floored or carpeted. Am I warm? Yes, I am warm, so I can't be outside. Have we lifted a carpet? Oh goodness, what on earth have we been up to in our drunken states?

I push my body up into a sitting position and use my hands to support me from collapsing as I battle dizziness. It's so dark I feel as though I still have my eyes closed, but I don't: they are wide open. Slowly, I move my hands around my body to try and find anything that would suggest where I am.

I find a wall, joined to another wall and move myself over to be supported. As I shuffle over, I put my hand in something wet. It's not water, it feels much thicker than water, but it's mixed with the grit of the dirty floor, which makes me shiver in disgust.

"Steven?" I call out with a very broken voice.

No response. I sweep my hair away from my face over the back of my head and feel my head is wet. Why is my head wet? Was it lying in that puddle of wet grit? No. In a flash, I remember exactly what happened. Someone hit me in the back of the head. What did they hit me with? Who was it? That's why my head hurts.

"Hello?" I call out, swallowing what little saliva I have left to try and rehydrate my voice.

There is no answer which is of no shock. What is going on? Where am I? I still can't see anything to give me any indication of where I might be. I stand up, keeping my hands above my head, and once I'm standing straight, I continue to put my hands up. My fingertips only just graze the roof, and I can feel that it is also solid concrete which makes me think I'm in some sort of shelter. I continue to trace my hands along the wall, moving them up and down, discovering more concrete walls as I do, and I come to another corner. Then another corner. But just as I want to give up hope, thinking I've been dropped into a concrete cube to die, I come across a door on the fourth wall. There's a thick metal handle which is appropriately heavy duty as the door itself is large and intimidating, and it is entirely made of metal. I finish my tour, and just past the door is where I found myself wakening: made evident by the small puddle of bloody grit.

I knock on the wall, checking the depth. I bang on the wall in frustration. "Hello?" I shout. "Hello!" I cry.

I slide down the wall where I'd just been sleeping, and my eyes sting as they fill with tears. I don't understand what is happening, and I have no information to try and piece together why I am trapped in here. I close my eyes and try to retrace my steps or try to remember what I could from before I was hit on the head last night. Was it even last night? I didn't feel tired, but I did feel a little rough, most likely from inhaling dirt and sleeping on concrete.

I remember being scared and someone hitting me on the head. I remember going into mum's room. I remember grabbing mum's shawl. I remember something strange. Yes! I remember pushing the back of the wardrobe and finding another landing with stairs. That was odd. Where did they lead? I can't remember anything else. I think that's when I got hit. Maybe I shouldn't have seen what I did, and that's why I'm here. But who hit me? Where did those stairs lead? This just can't be real. Surely this must be some sort of illustrious and vivid drunken dream. This is not a real-life situation; it's a scene from a film that I wouldn't choose to watch because it is so far from farfetched that the plot begs belief.

Sat in the dead silence that the concrete provided, I was thinking about every little thing that happened over the weekend that didn't seem quite right. Why was there a handprint on the outside of our patio doors? It was not there before because I would have noticed it. Was that done by the same person who hit me on the head? Has that person hurt my family? Oh god, Steven. My family. Are they ok? I don't know anything, and it's making me angry. Also, did Ellie and I actually hear a person in that room downstairs on the first day, and if we did hear a person, was it them that hit me? Is someone hurting Steven and my family right now? Will I be able to escape? Am I going to die here?

My being here in this room with my head bleeding is implausible. I refuse to consider the rationality of it. I am a shrewd person, but I will not allow myself to be seduced by this sick fantasy that is not real life. Any moment now, my family will appear, and Steven will kiss me, and everything will return to ordinary reality. That is what's going to happen. Isn't it?

I lay down and curl up, replaying the weekend events over and over in my mind. The isolation of the lodge. The breathing coming from the impenetrable room. The handprint on the outside of the window. The lack of curtains. The damaged boat. The noise that came from upstairs as though someone else was in the house, which I now knew to be true. The freaky hidden landing and staircase behind the wardrobe. The person that hit me on the head. The fact that I'm in a solid concrete room in complete darkness. I could be anywhere.

I close my eyes.

I get a fright when I think I hear a noise. I must have fallen asleep in my distress. With my eyes open as wide as they will go, I try and scan the room for any evidence to suggest I did hear a noise or that there is a way out of this nightmare that I'd previously overlooked. Obviously, there's not, and I feel stupid for even allowing myself to think positively about my situation. I pick myself up and wipe the dust off my face, which has gotten into my eyes and made them itchy. Using the wall as a navigation aid, I found the door and tried to see if I could open it. Shaking it and using all of my strength didn't help. It is solid.

The same sound I thought I had heard when I woke up sounded again. It was like a strong clap.

"Hello?" I turned round in a panic to face the pitch black room. "Is someone there?"

Did someone come in while I was sleeping? Or was someone in the room all along? I hold my breath to try and listen for any sign of life, but the room is so soundproofed that I can't hear anything. I put my hands in front of me and walk forward, toward the other side of the room without using the walls for support. Maybe there's a way out in the centre of the room; why did I not check that before? I take little steps trying to avoid hurting myself by falling or tripping.

I reach the other side of the room after coming across nothing else on my journey, so what on earth was that noise? Then, with fervent conviction, the noise came again like a hard ball falling on the concrete, the clap of hands, or the pop of cling film.

"Hello?" I made a last-ditch attempt to determine if there was a person there. I listened as hard as I could, and I thought I heard something shuffle on the ground. That better not be a rat.

"I know someone is there. What the fuck is going on?" I shouted in a panic at, not wanting to see or feel a rat at my feet.

"Calm down, Kyle." A voice replied with a chuckle from across the room where the door was.

What? Did I imagine that? "Who are you? What's going on?" I was sweating, and my heart was racing. Someone else is in this room with me. How have they been avoiding me? Can they see me? Where are they? Did they lock me in here? Are they trapped in here too?

"Are you going to hurt me?" My panic makes me cry, and I sob while grabbing at the wall with my fingers. I've found a loose lump of concrete in the wall. As I audibly panic, I wobble it out.

A Killer

If something doesn't happen soon, I'll have to leave because if all has gone to plan, then the three of them should be outside waiting for me for the next step of the plan. Or maybe they've used their initiative and continued, but I highly doubt that. I've been stuck in here with this poof for far too long for nothing to have happened. I take off the goggles for a second because they're getting quite tight on my head, and it's not entirely satisfying to stare at a red coloured un-moving shape for about an hour, before walking towards him and giving him a shove with my foot.

He stirred. Excellent. I put the goggles back on in anticipation of the fun beginning. I want him to beg. I want him to break down and cry and plead with anyone to save him. He takes far too long to wake up, so I start to move toward him to give him a brush or a push, but he starts to move his arm, narrowly missing my foot. Come on. Get up.

I watch him slowly sit up, and I feel myself smiling. I'm a little nervous now; it's becoming real. I promised the guys outside that this was the family for us, but a tiny part of me had grown to like them.

"Steven?" Kyle pathetically croaks as he looks around, disorientated.

Just like that, I lose my nerves. I might have grown to like them, but that didn't stop them from being disgusting excuses for humans, making a mockery of our species and race. He makes me sick calling out for his fairy boyfriend. He wouldn't save him anyway, just scream like a girl and run. It has made my skin crawl thinking about how they dare to call each other husband, completely destroying the sanctity of marriage, which should only be between a man and a woman. The way God intended.

I have an ear to ear grin as I watch the Nancy boy realise his head is bleeding. His little red outline even looks scared, and I can just imagine the look on his tragic Trixie face. It felt so good to hit him, I wish I could have hit him harder, but then we wouldn't be able to have fun like this, would I?

"Hello?" Kyle hilariously tries to clear his throat and sound confident. Keep trying, mate. There isn't a hope in hell for you to sound masculine to someone who knows you like to bugger. I shiver in contempt for what this piece of scum is. As he stands up, a shot of adrenaline runs through my body; I am going to have so much fun. I have been dreaming about tonight for months. Contemplating every possible move anyone could make and how we can ensure whatever they do to try and stop us, doesn't succeed.

Kyle is touching the roof, and I prepare to move. I can tell he's going to start exploring the room. My plan for this moment had just been to continually scare him into psychological stress, but I am not entirely sure how I am going to do that. Yet. He starts to trace his hands along the room's perimeter, running them laterally down each wall, almost chasing me as I precariously walk around the room a few steps in front of him. As I pass the door, I can see a red figure on the stairs outside. Who's that? It better be one of us and not part of the family. I move into the middle of the room and turn to watch Kyle padding around the door with his hands trying to find a way to unlock or open it. I have to silence myself as I laugh at the little rat panicking.

"Hello?" He shouts. Dammit, did he hear me laugh? I haven't had a chance to have any fun with the little runt yet. "Hello!" He starts crying. Maybe he didn't hear me, then. He's just a pathetic excuse; he is not even trying to open the door. I locked the door; it's solid and not going anywhere, but I expected him to spend longer trying to find a way to open it before he gave up like the little girl he is. Leaning against the wall, sobbing like a pitiful girl's blouse, I hate him. I want to run my knife clean into him, but thou shalt not kill.

He slides down the wall and hangs his head in his hands. I surreptitiously move closer to him and blow towards his face. He doesn't even flinch; he is so self-involved and self-centred that he isn't aware of his surroundings. The fact that he hasn't even realised I'm in this twelve by twelve-foot concrete room is reason enough to torture him, quite frankly. He moves slowly, lying down and curls up into the foetal position and half of me is riled with rage; why is he not trying to find a way out? The other half of me has to stop myself from laughing at how much of a waste of space he's proving himself to be.

I think he's gone to sleep because he's gone quiet and seems very still. I did hit him pretty hard on the head; what if he has a concussion? What if he's dead already? You're not supposed to let someone who has a concussion go to sleep, right? Balls. I walk over and nudge his body with my foot again, but he doesn't flinch or stir. Dammit. I place my hands close to his ear and bring them together in a brisk move to give a sharp clap sound. That seems to have done the trick as Kyle moves. Excellent. I skulk backwards to evade him again. Clapping is good. My clap sounded piercing but leaden in this dead room, less like a clap and more like a gunshot.

Kyle gets up lethargically and goes straight to the door. He has a good old feel around the door and even tries shaking it, banging on it and feeling around for the hinges. It's sad, really, how naïve he is to think he'll ever be able to get out of that door. It's about a foot thick. We hit the jackpot when we came across this room, really. Having planned to just use the back of the gang's van. This was much more fun; there was room to move around, and we didn't tie Kyle up for added amusement.

Kyle was always going to be the first one we tortured, but we didn't expect him to make it quite so easy for us to obtain. Claire is supposed to be next, but I'm having too much fun with Kyle; I should probably go soon to help. We are going to tie Claire up and lock her in her bathroom. She's just as pathetic as Kyle. A repulsive whore who is married to an immigrant. The thought is enough to make you sick.

I'm bored of watching this little dick-sucker scramble around the doorway for a way out, and I'm thinking about how we are going to make Claire cry and beg for us to not hurt her. Part of me can't believe it's all going to plan and finally happening after months of dreaming and planning. I bring my hands up and clap them together to give another deep and harsh sound like before. I have to stop myself from laughing as I watch Kyle turn round in a single spin of gay alarm.

"Hello?" He asked the room, his voice shaking. "Is someone there?" I want to punch him in his stupid ugly face and slide my knife into his ribs to let him know, yes, someone is here. But instead, I take a step back and watch the dumb fuck quiver in fear. He puts his arms in front of him and walks through the middle of the room; what is he expecting to find? What would he do if he found another person? Scream like a girl and cry. As Kyle moves to the other side of the room, I move towards the door where the figure is still on the other side. It must be one of us waiting for me.

I turn round and clap again, this time hearing a tiny echo, probably caused by the big metal door. I'm ready to push Kyle's buttons and break him just before leaving. But, again, right on cue, he turns around. There is no hiding from the fact that someone else is in the room with him now; the clap has moved position, and there is no other explanation.

"Hello?" He calls out. Again. I'm getting painfully bored of his pathetic shaky voice. As I pull the key to the door out of my pocket, I step into something wet. What is that? Is that Kyle's blood? Dammit.

"I know someone is there. What the fuck is going on?" Kyle shouted in a relatively aggressive tone, and I was rather impressed, or I would be if he now didn't start hyperventilating.

"Calm down, Kyle." I replied while trying to not laugh. Kyle doesn't say anything and appears to be frozen in shock. The fact that I spoke has probably freaked him out. Excellent.

"Who are you? What's going on?" Oh yeah, I'll just tell you who I am and that I am here with my friends outside to try and kill you through fear and torture. I'll just reveal everything to you since you asked. Stupid queer.

"Are you going to hurt me?" He asked while crying, still apparently frozen on the spot.

"Yes. We are going to hurt you. We are going to hurt you so much you're going to wish you were dead like your faggot friend, Steven." I said menacingly while pushing the key into the lock.

"What?" Again, with the crying. "Steven's dead?"

"Whoops, maybe I shouldn't have told you that." I laughed as I turned to open the door and leave. I unlocked the door as quietly as I could. I heard Kyle running for me.

"Don't bother trying anything, faggot." I say as I turn with my knife in my hand.

Ellie

As the door shuts behind me, my heart starts to race. What am I doing? My family must be crazy trusting me on this. I stand here for a moment, leaning on the door, just contemplating what I'm about to do before actually undertaking the challenge. If I get caught, what happens? Will they kill me? Probably. I hear Steven start wedging the door closed with the bed slats, and I know that is my cue to leave; or go back in, but if this is one of our only chances out of here, then I have to try.

I scan the upper lounge for any sign of movement and listen for any breathing. I have no idea what I'd do if I was to come across someone right now. Probably run and hide somewhere, but that wouldn't be very clever. I look down at my hand and remember I took one of the chair legs with me. It's in my hand. I'm holding it. Jeez, Ellie, pull yourself together. I raise the leg above my head and embrace it like a baseball bat. At least I have a plan of action now.

Listening intently to the lodge, I can't hear much except the odd noise or muffled voice coming from mum and dad's room that was now our battlement. I peered over the edge of the bannister, and all I saw was darkness and shadows; luckily, no shadows appeared to be moving, so I began my descent to the ground floor. As I stepped on the centre stair, I commended myself for how calm I had remained thus far. Oh my goodness, I just used the word thus in a sentence, and I used it correctly. I can't wait to tell everyone. Jackson will be impressed.

Once I'm on the ground floor, I give it a scan, but I have no idea what I'm looking for. These people have been evading our sights in this lodge for two days, and if our theory of there being three of them is correct, we are still to find the third, and they could very well be hiding in plain sight of me. I edge closer to the door and look into Kyle and Steven's bedroom. I can see the two figures out the front through the patio doors, staring up at the bedroom. What they are doing doesn't make sense. They know where we are, so why are they just staring at us? It's not as though the room is impenetrable - as much as

Steven has tried to make it so. The only reason I can think of is that they are waiting for their third, who could be with Kyle right now.

I slide my body along the wall past the stairs and feel the sweat streaming down my face and back as I approach the top of the lower stairs. I hold my breath to try and hear something, but all I can hear is my own heartbeat, which I'm now conscious is overpoweringly loud and will give away where I am. I stand, rooted to the floor, take a deep breath and slowly peer around the corner and down the second flight of stairs.

There's a figure at the bottom of them. Fuck, did they see me? My breathing feels out of control. Before I allow myself to start to panic, I remember I have the upper hand; I'm standing at the top of the stairs with a weapon. As I listen to try and determine what this figure is doing, it seems as though they are not moving. I look round the corner again, this time a little more confidently and spot that they are actually facing towards the door that I was unable to open. I knew that room was not right. Why are they staring at it?

Is this leg hard enough to knock them out? I think it might be, but should I take something else for good measure? What would I take? The knives I've come to get are downstairs. I decide that if I alert them to someone being up here, I will swing the leg in their face at full force as they come up the stairs. That should work. Oh my Christ, my heart reminds me that it's there by punching me from the inside, and I notice my sweat has started to drip onto the floor. I grab one of the candles from the sideboard at the sofas and walk over to the corner, just behind the stairs and I underarm throw the candle as far in the kitchen area as I can. It definitely sounded as though someone would be in the kitchen, but it was a relatively small sound, and I initially feel a little disheartened until I hear the figure take their first step up the stairs. What have I done? I've exposed myself to a sadistic killer, and I expect myself to be able to fend them off on a level playing field. Am I crazy? I feel like my body is a step closer to implosion with every step the figure takes. I feel impatient, then petrified, then remorseful, then confused; then I see the figure's foot on the floor and in slow motion, as the figure pulls themself up onto the ground floor; I swing the chair leg I had been holding aloft, for what felt like such a long time, with all of my body. I think the leg hits the figure's head, and I am shocked at how smoothly it goes, like a spoon going through water, then honey. It's not until the leg bounces off the wall that I stop swinging, but the slow motion continues as I hear the figure take a deep inhale of breath and choke on their breath in shock. I turn round the corner and watch the figure fly down the stairs and end in a contorted shape, having broken the bottom three stairs with the land.

I stand for a moment in shock at what I have just done. I don't want the figure to move, but I also need the figure to move. I can't have hurt them so much that they are... dead? Fuck. What have I done? I'm frozen on the spot, and I'm scared one of the other figures may have heard the crash. With a shiver up my spine, I am pushed off the spot by my own body. I rush over to the window and spy that the two figures are still outside, so I run to the stairs and creep down. When I reach the figure's body, I place my hand on their head and apologise. I feel awful for what I have done, but this person would have done it to my family. I think.

Staring at the figure, I start to cry. "I'm so sorry." I sob. I am genuinely sorry. I feel sick. Was this necessary? I can't bear to look at this poor, broken body any longer, so I rush past and hop into the games room.

I run over to the cupboard where I found the bag of knives before and try to open it. It's locked. Of course, it is; of course, nothing is going to be straightforward about tonight. But, thinking about it, what is the time? I sneak past the crumpled body on the stairs and into my bedroom to grab my little tool kit. All things considered, I think I'm pretty safe to do this as if someone else had been in the house, they would have come as soon as their accomplice hit the floor. But I'm not thinking about what I did. So stop it, Ellie. Stop it. I find my tool kit and run back through to pick the cupboard's lock. Within a matter of seconds, the crystal clear click signals my success, and I swing the door open. Someone has definitely been in here since I was.

I rummage through the cupboard to get to the bag, which is at the bottom, when I hear a click. What was that? I then hear a long creak like that of a rusty door hinge. Seriously? I can't catch a break. I can hear someone breathing heavily like they're out of breath, and they make incredulous noises over the body at the bottom of the stairs. Christ, there's a fourth person. How many more could there be? I step as quietly as I can into the cupboard and pull the door as close to closed as possible without letting it click shut, which would make a noise. A fourth figure comes into the room, and I can see they are holding one of the knives I'd seen in the bag next to me this morning. I squeeze my eyes shut. If they've come to get more of their stuff, I'm done. Let them take me. I can't do this anymore.

When I open my eyes and hear the figure climbing the stairs, I take a moment to remind myself of how strong I am. I am a strong woman, and I am doing so well, given the circumstances. Then, pushing open the cupboard door, I grab the bag with everything in it and skulk out of the room as I spy the figure round the corner slyly towards the front door and staircase.

However, what makes my heart skip a beat is that the door that had remained locked and wouldn't open for me was now stood wide open and was revealing a pitch black space that I absolutely did not care to explore. This was where the fourth person came from, but I couldn't see anything inside it; how did they see it inside? That's clearly what the person I hit was waiting on. His friend and accomplice joining the merciless gang.

I was being pulled into this space. Curiosity killed the cat, mum would be saying right now. There were two doors. The hall door that I unlocked and a thick metal door that was clearly the reason why the hall door wouldn't budge. Where did it lead? I placed my hand inside and touched the wall to see if there was a light switch. I couldn't feel anything on either side, only a cool stone wall. I look down and see a large puddle of blood, but before thinking about that, I suddenly can hear voices. Shit. I look into mine and Jackson's bedroom and see two people walking past the window outside, speaking in hushed voices. Fuck. I like to sleep with the windows open, which is lucky as I now have a warning of them coming. Where are they going? They disappear past the windows, and I don't want to stay to find out.

Being as trepid as possible, I mount the stairs one at a time, placing both feet flat before taking my next step. The bag weighs heavy on my back, and I definitely feel like there are extra things in here since I looked this morning. Plus, my arms are growing pretty tired of holding this chair leg above my head.

Once I am at the top of the stairs, my heart starts to beat me up from inside again. What if someone is waiting for me like I was waiting for their friend? What if I'm walking into a trap? What if they have already got to everyone upstairs? What if I'm about to die after all I've just been through?

"Ellie?" A voice comes from the shadows in the corner of the room. My eyes instantly water, and I feel myself give in like I did when I was hiding in the cupboard downstairs.

"Yes. Just get it over with, you fucker." I bring the chair leg down, hanging my arms and my head as I sob.

Shelley & Claire

As soon as the door clicks shut, I regret letting my baby leave. What are we letting her do?

"Get her back. I can't let her go." I call to Steven as I put Rubeus down and run towards the door.

"Mum, let her go. She said she knows what she's doing, and if she isn't back in twenty minutes, Mike will go get her." Claire grabbed me and held me tight as I cried a little. I knew she was right, but it was still difficult to let your youngest child go to her possible death. Maybe I'm being dramatic, but we don't know anything, and my baby boy is missing.

"She's going to be fine, Shell. I wouldn't want to get on the bad side of her on a good day, let alone just now." Steven said in an attempt to cheer me up, but the truth is there was no way I could even think about cheer right now. In our situation.

Trying not to be rude, I smiled at the kids, picked up Rubeus and walked over to Graham. He was sat on the floor with his legs crossed and was watching the figures outside. We are taking it in turns so we don't get disorientated. He put his hand on my thigh as I knelt down beside him, and he squeezed it so that I knew he understood and felt the same way as I did. Without turning around, I could hear Steven and Mike begin to put the bed slats in the door gaps to prevent it from being opened by anyone on the other side. Ellie was officially on her own. They didn't put the heavy dresser back where it had been in front of the door, so it was easier to open for when Ellie returns.

The room fell silent again. Silent but loud. Loud with thoughts.

What the hell is behind that cupboard? Last night when I saw the door close, someone was in there. Rubeus knew it, and I couldn't believe I'd been so ignorant to a malevolent stranger being in the same room as me. We decided to block it up as best we could using the remaining furniture in the room and bathroom in case they tried to get in from there, and part of me hoped they tried. I'd love for one of them to come in. I'd fly at them.

While we were sitting in our silence, there was a small, muffled bang followed by a slightly louder, muffled crash. I look at Claire, and her eyes tell me to stay calm.

"Did they hear anything, dad?" Claire asked as we all looked quizzically at each other, wondering what Ellie was doing.

"They didn't move a muscle." Graham replied without averting his gaze.

"When I was sitting outside earlier, I couldn't hear a thing that was going on inside."

"But if there is a third person inside the house, they most certainly did hear that." I tried to control my breathing, attempting not to panic.

-

I can see mum starting to panic, and if I'm frank with myself, I'm using every ounce of my being to stop myself from crumbling.

"We wait until the twenty minutes are over, and if she's not back by then, Mike will go and find her." I squeeze mum for support. "Dad, is it maybe time you and I swapped now?" I asked to hint that mum might need his undivided attention right now in order to remain calm.

"I'm ok to hold on a few more minutes, darling."

"No, dad. Let me take over, and you and mum go and sit on the covers."

He got the hint and apologetically looked at me before the three of them sat down on the pillows and covers in the corner. I sat down on the legless chair and crossed my legs over it, getting comfy. I locked my eyes on the two figures, whom I hated with a burning passion inside, and noted that they had not moved from where I remembered them to be. What was their game?

Above my head, we had successfully written a short note reading, 'GET POLICE. DANGER.' to Jackson in lipsticks and make up across the window for when we see his car coming up the drive. According to Steven, the figures didn't move when we were writing the message and appeared to laugh. I scan the area for any sign of the third person joining, and the fog is most certainly thinning. I look to the driveway to see how much is visible, but I spot a lot more than I want to be seeing.

"Mike. Steven." I call the boys over to subtly show them what I see before telling mum and dad. They walk over, and I point to the driveway.

"Is that..." Steven starts with a shake in his voice.

"Yes." I whisper. "They must have got him first."

"Oh god."

Neither Mike nor Steven are helpful to the situation and remain stunned in silence. Our only escape route is now gone. All of our hopes have been scuppered. We are not getting out of this lodge. When we ran to Steven's car, they might have been mere footsteps from us. When I heard someone shuffling in front of me earlier on while I was outside, could that have been Jackson? Could I have helped him?

"Mum, dad. You might want to come over here and see this." I think I'm in shock because I sound entirely emotionless.

"What are they doing?" Mum asks, assuming the figures are up to something.

"Nothing." I reply. "It's what they have done."

Down the drive, around thirty metres away and only ten metres back from Steven and Kyle's car sat Jackson's car with the driver's door wide open. The lights were off, and the car wasn't running, but there was no sign of Jackson anywhere. What made the whole situation much worse was that directly behind Jackson's car was a large black van. The van's passenger side was open and inside was too dark to determine if anything was inside. These fuckers must have caught Jackson just as he was leaving for the shop, and that's why he has still not returned.

-

"Well. We're up shit creek." I said, feeling ultimately defeated.

"Mum." Claire said, and I couldn't tell if she was telling me off or asking for my help.

"To be fair, we've been treading in shit creek all night." Mike offered, which made Claire give him a helpless glare.

I looked to Graham, who looked back at me, completely lost. We were all feeling deflated and like we couldn't go on putting up a fight or defending ourselves much longer. Poor Jackson. Poor Kyle. Maybe poor Ellie. Goodness, what do I say to Ellie if she comes back? How can I even think 'if' she comes back? She will come back. She will. But when she does, we have to show her that Jackson might not be coming to save us after all, and she'll have to accept that these people don't just have Kyle, but they have Jackson too.

"How did you not see that earlier?" I ask Graham.

"I was solely focussed on our tormentors." He defended himself. "I didn't take my eyes off of them once."

"Well, maybe you should have, and that way, we could have stopped our baby girl from going out straight into danger, not knowing what would happen." I am angry, and it's not at Graham. It's not, but I can't stop myself from shouting at him.

"Mum, this is not dads or any of our faults." Claire stood up and hugged me. Graham joined in, and Steven and Mike added on.

"I love you so much. But I'm just so scared."

Everyone let go of me, and Graham took my arms.

"Love me tender. Love me...true. Hmm, hmm, hmm, hmm, hmm." Steven started to sing but ended up humming, and as he did, Claire and Mike joined in too. Graham and I danced while part of our beautiful and perfect family hummed our song. They repeatedly hummed the chorus, but it was perfect; I could feel myself filling with energy. I looked at Graham and kissed his cheek before letting go of his embrace and walking to the window.

"Thank you." I said sincerely while looking out at the figures outside.

They're gone. "Where have they gone?" I ask and point to where they had been. "Did anyone see them move?"

-

"I wasn't paying attention to them after I spotted Jackson's car and the van behind it." I admit that I am at fault since it was my time to watch the figures. "I'm so sorry."

"Don't be sorry. They must be on the move for a reason." Mum showed a little kindness towards me, which I wasn't expecting.

"Do you think they saw Ellie?" Mike asked.

Oh, Christ. They saw Ellie, and they have gone to get her.

"Should I go and see if she's ok?"

"Not yet, Mike, my love." Mum seemed as though she was concocting a plan. I hope she was because my heart hadn't raced quite like it is now for at least twenty minutes, and I was ready for some sort of hope.

"Graham, do you think you can get that van started without keys?"

"Of course. Why?"

"Claire, do you think you can keep your father calm and return here with help or the police?"

"Yes, of course. I'll phone them as soon as we get a bar of signal." I understood precisely what mum was thinking.

"Ok. We just need to get you to the van without anyone noticing." Mum continued with her plan.

"We need a distraction." Dad said.

"We'll wait for Ellie to get back."

Kyle

If I could see anything right now, I'd imagine everything would be blurry. If I could hear anything right now, I doubt I'd be able to distinguish sounds over the whistling currently going through me. My body feels stiff, like when a limb has gone numb, and you are scared to move it for fear of hurting yourself. I'm still squeezing the rock in my hand, and I still have someone on top of me, and I still don't know where I am, and I still don't know how I am going to get out, and I still don't know if it will be safe when I get out.

There's only one way to find out, I guess. I place two fingers on this person's neck, and I can feel a faint pulse. Do I hit them one more time and hope the pulse disappears? Kyle, what are you thinking? No. I move to push them off, and as I do, a blinding pain immobilises me in my side. I try desperately not to scream because if I do, I might stir whoever inflicted this pain on me, but it is so concentrated I let out a whimper. I trace around my body using my right hand, where the pain is now emanating spectacularly. As I slowly edge my fingers closer to the root of the pain, I can't help but cry; I know what I'm going to find; I felt it happen.

Having found the rip in my top and feeling the wealth of blood in its vicinity, I have discovered quite enough to ease my suspicion. I've been stabbed. I can't believe it. I have been stabbed. This sort of thing doesn't happen to ordinary people. It happens to people on the news and in TV shows and films.

Using my right hand again, I find this person's belt and frantically try to get it off without moving them. Once I have it, I rip a sleeve off of my top and place it over the wound; I wrap it around my middle and buckle it tight to calm the bleeding; and, hopefully, dull the pain. It surprisingly seems successful, and I pull myself onto my knees, using the back corner of the room for added support, and then lay the person flat. I think we landed in a pile in the back corner during the scuffle, but I need to find a way out of here, and I need to find it before this person comes to. They seem to have a mask, or something, on. Wait, what is that? I pull off what feels like binoculars and bring them level with my eyes. No. Absolutely not. I refuse to believe that someone has gone to as much trouble as this person has in order to hurt my family and me. In disbelief, I put the goggle binocular thing on and look around. I can see the shape of the person who lays in front of me in a light orange. I look around the room, and I can slightly make out the shape of the door in a light blue, and beyond the door, I can see another figure who is a warmer orange in a standing position.

While trying to process the level of commitment these people have adhered to, I awkwardly feel around the body for more information or a key. I peel off part of their balaclava and feel stubble which confirms my notion that he is a man, and I get disheartened when I find nothing else on his body.

Where is the knife? I can't have him coming to and attacking me again. Although I have his night-vision goggles/body-heat goggles, so I do have the upper hand. But to be on the safe side, I run my hand along the floor around us both until I find the knife, which feels rather brutal. As I hold it in my hand, I feel sick. I have been stabbed. Someone wanted to kill me. There are people who want to hurt my family and me. This is too much to take in. I put my hand over my wound and can feel more blood than before. No, no, no. This can't be happening. I miss Steven. My beautiful, intelligent and caring bear. I don't even know if he's okay. What if he isn't? I couldn't do anything without him.

I finally put down the rock I'd been squeezing in my left hand by throwing it into the opposite corner of the room. I grip the knife tightly in my right hand and pull myself up to stand. While I am allowing my body to get used to the pain, I notice that the orange figure on the other side of the door was now lying down and appeared to be in a slightly contorted shape. What is going on?

Hobbling over to the door, I begin to get breathless, and when I make it to the door, I take a moment to catch my breath, and as I do, I squeeze the patch of material I had used to seal where I'd been stabbed. It drips blood onto the floor, and each drop of blood sounds like thunder in my head.

Taking a deep breath and holding it, I try to open the door. It moves more than it did before, and I get a shock as it does. Why is it moving this time? I get excited and hopeful, but as I do, I can feel my heart rate increase, but I don't want that to happen because it will make me bleed more. I roll my hand over the door and find a key. The person tormenting me must have put the key in just as I attacked him.

Turning the key, I feel the door loosening in front of me, and a dart of adrenaline courses its way through my body. I pull it towards me, and I have to lean on it to push it further open as it is too heavy for me to pull at the moment. It opens to reveal another door, and I can see it because there is light seeping through the edges of the door frame. I reach for where I think the handle is; I pull it open and take off the goggles, struggling to see anything as my eyes adjust to something that's not pitch black, nothingness. The door creaks awfully as it opens, and I realise exactly where I am. I'm staring at the staircase that leads to the basement floor of the lodge; to the left of me is the games room and to the right is Ellie's room. The figure I'd seen through the door was now lying on the bottom few stairs, their body broken and disfigured. I have no idea what has happened, and I don't care to wait around and find out; I want to get to anyone in my family. Popping into both rooms downstairs, I see no sign of movement or life, so I try to hike the stairs; as quietly as I can, considering my pain.

Once I mount the top of the stairs, I am slapped with an overwhelming rush of fear. What If I come across someone else? Why are all the lights off? Are my family hiding, or have they been taken away? What if the guy downstairs wakes up and comes to get me? I'm too weak to fight him off; I wouldn't survive round two. I round the corner into the lounge area using the wall as support, and I walk towards the corner of the lounge, next to the window where it is masked, entirely in darkness. I can stand there and wear the goggles to see if there is anyone else here.

I reach the corner, and I do everything I can to slow my breathing and heart rate down. I am completely supported by the walls right now, and I loosen the belt for a moment while I take off the ripped sleeve from my wound. I tear off my other sleeve, replace it on my side, and tighten the belt around it. I have controlled my breathing until now, but I'm starting to shake, and I can hear the uncontrollable quiver in my breath. I begin to scan the area for any sign of life, but as I do so, I can see a person coming up the stairs from where I just came. The person ascending the stairs is much redder than the orange glow of my attacker and the even paler hue of the body on the stairs. They look smaller, but that could be because I'm further away from them. What if it's the man who held me hostage? He looks like he's holding something above his head by the shape of his glow. What if it isn't him? Where has this person come from? I shake my head and squeeze my eyes to stop myself from crying.

As the red figure reaches the top of the stairs, I hold my breath. There is no way I am not getting to Steven; after all I have just been through. I'll be as quiet as possible, and they'll just walk on past me because I need to milk this stabbing for years to come. I will milk this stabbing. I will.

But. Wait. Is that?

"Ellie?" I can't believe it. As she turns the corner, I recognise her shape, and I pull off the goggles to make sure. Yes. It really is her.

"Yes. Just get it over with, you fucker." She brings the bat down from above her head and sobs.

"Jellybean, no. It's me. It's Kyle."

All

I still have no idea what I am going to say to Ellie when she comes back. We are all planning ahead and feeling slightly positive about what we have to do now, but when Ellie finds out that Jackson is in the same position as Kyle; will she feel as empowered as she did when she nominated herself to go and get the bag of things from the basement, or will she just crumble and fall apart?

Steven should be the one to tell her. Not me. I definitely have very little compassion, as evidenced by how I treated Mike after we lost the baby. Steven is in the same position, and he is closer to her because she visits them much more often than she sees me.

"I still think Steven should tell Ellie when she gets here."

"I'll support her and hold her up, but I can't tell her: that has to be you or your mum, Claire."

"I can't tell her. She'll end up blaming me for everything that's happened."

"We would never let that happen, Shell. None of this is anyone's fault." Mike assuaged.

"It has to be you, Claire, baby. You'll set off the smallest reaction in her if you do it." Mum said, coming over and hugging me. "If I do it, she will get angry; if dad does it, she will get angry, and if Steven does it, she will fall into helpless despair."

"Great, then Mike can do it." I half-joke, which the group acknowledge.

"No joking until we are all safe and out of the woods. Literally." Dad said as he continued scanning outside.

What will I even say?

Ellie, we think it's not only your brother who might be dead but also your boyfriend. No.

Ellie, thank you so much for being so brave and going to get us things to help us escape and as a reward, come look at this; your boyfriend's car never made it out of the drive, and we think he is in grave danger. No.

Ellie, baby, you're so beautiful. You will find someone else. Jackson wasn't as perfect as he could be. No.

Ellie, maybe your boyfriend's car did make it out of the drive, and he led these people here in their van. But that wouldn't explain all the goings on over the past two days. Jeez, Claire, pull yourself together. Jackson is in danger. He's not evil.

Ellie, we love you so much. We are all here for you, and we are so sorry to have to tell you this. But we think Jackson has been taken by these people like Kyle has been too. His car is still on the driveway, and the driver's door is open, which suggests he was taken before he even left for the shops. We are going to get help, though. We have half a plan, and we will be back for Kyle and Jackson.

-

While we wait for the final minute of Ellie's given twenty to lapse in our tense silence, I hear something that sounds slightly clumpy coming from outside. Rubeus's ears prick up, and he hops along to the door. I'd love to have his blissful ignorance right now. He turns to me, and I put my finger to my lips and hush him. He is such a good boy; he understands not to make a sound. I look at Graham, who is intently watching outside, and then I look at the door where Steven and Mike have already positioned themselves in a striking position with chair legs above their head. Claire is looking at me with fear in her eyes. I get up and place my ear to the wall to try and distinguish what the sound is. It doesn't come very often, and if I was to guess, it would be someone dragging themselves up the stairs. Is it Ellie? Is she hurt?

Claire taps me on the shoulder and mouths, "Ellie?"

If it is Ellie, when she reaches the door, she will hum. We wait anxiously. I can't hear anything yet. I'm starting to panic; what if she is hurt and can't hum, what if it's not her, what if it is her, but if she hums, she'll give away where she is? I push my ear hard against the wall and slide it along towards the door. The clumping has stopped, but now I hear something else. It sounds like breathlessness. Is it Ellie? Is it Jackson? Is it Kyle? Is it one of the figures? If it is the latter, then I feel somewhat more confident about outsmarting them until Graham and Claire get help.

Claire picks Rubeus up and takes him into the bathroom, where he is distracted by his bone, and returns to put her hands on my shoulders for support. We trepidatiously await a sign to signal what is going on. Silence.

-

"Watch as soon as they open the door. I'll be forgotten about." I whisper to Kyle as I help him take the stairs one at a time, as quietly as we can. I was incredibly happy to have found Kyle; I was so worried about him, and I, sadistically, couldn't wait to hear what he had been through.

"Oh, shut up; they'll be ecstatic to see us both. I've been held hostage, tormented and stabbed, and you've been heroic and killed someone."

"Don't say that. Please, don't. I really can't have everyone knowing yet." Every time I thought of that person on the stairs, I felt a sharp pain inside, which made me feel overcome with nausea.

"Sorry." Kyle knew I wasn't going to deal well with what I did but to be honest, I didn't know exactly how I felt about it because I hadn't processed what had happened yet. All I was thinking about was getting upstairs, barricading ourselves in and fending for ourselves until Jackson returned with help.

Thinking about Jackson made me smile. I miss him. He will definitely have been back by now, and because I've not heard a calamity, I presume our plan for him to read our message has been successful.

We reach the top of the stairs, and Kyle is so breathless I start to worry if his wound is more severe than he made it out to be downstairs. At that moment, we both hear a slight thud come from downstairs. Kyle looks at me, and I shake my head to say I didn't know what it could be. There's another slightly lighter thud moments later, but with our attention now focussed on the source, it sounds as though they came from Kyle and Steven's room. We didn't look in there before we ascended the stairs, and now my sweats have returned. It's as though Kyle completely distracted me from the fact that we are in grave danger. I know that I need to hum for the door to get opened, but I don't want to hum and give away where Kyle and I are because what if the door doesn't get opened in time and what if I just have them open the door so they can be attacked?

If they were in the bedroom the whole time, why didn't they come out when we were downstairs? If they weren't in the bedroom the whole time, where have they come from?

-

Are you for real? I am not in the mood for another stab. I look at Ellie and try to telepathically scream at her to do what she needs to do to get us to safety. She nods and starts to hum. Humming? She's humming. Oh, Christ, she's making noise and telling whoever is thudding in my bedroom exactly where we are.

While she is humming, something is happening inside mum and dad's bedroom, but from inside the bedroom at the bottom of the stairs, a figure appears, and another joins them. They look up at Ellie and me from the bottom of the stairs before revealing their weapons. One has a giant bat, and one has a knife the size of his arm. My heart can't take much more of this. I can see them smile through their balaclavas, and I am filled with a burning hatred inside.

"Quickly!" Ellie shouts as the figures start to ascend the stairs.

I shock myself by, without even thinking, grabbing the side table just behind Ellie and pushing it down the stairs. It stunts the figures for only a moment as they move aside to let it pass them. I grab the pictures from the walls and start throwing them at the figures.

"Kyle!" Mum screams from behind me. The bedroom door is open, and inside I see everyone. Ellie grabs me and pulls me into the room, where I fall to the ground and scream in pain because the adrenaline of fighting off the figures made me forget I was hurt. I watch Steven, dad and Mike block up the door, and I can hear the figures banging on the door as they do so. Mum is kneeling at my head, and I look up at her as I squirm; she's crying. I feel cold. I have to close my eyes.

-

The figures keep trying to bang on the door and move over to the wall when the door is impenetrable. But the lodge is well built, and they don't seem to be able to break through. Finally, after around thirty seconds of trying, it goes quiet. Silent. I turn to see my baby brother bleeding and mum and Steven crying over him. No way. No.

I fall to my knees and grab Steven's hand.

"He's not dead." Mum announces through tears. "I think he's just passed out."

"What happened?" I ask Ellie in a state of shock while still squeezing Steven's hand.

"I don't know. He said he'd tell me when we got somewhere safe."

"Where did you find him?" Mum asked, kissing Kyle's head and loosening the belt on his stomach to examine his wound.

"On my way back upstairs, he was hiding in the lounge. I thought I was a dead woman. We found each other, and on our way up the stairs, someone came into the house through Kyle and Steven's bedroom."

"Where had he been?" Mum asked before retching at Kyle's wound.

"I don't know, guys." Ellie snapped. "I was completely on my own until two minutes ago when we found each other in the lounge. We thought it better to get to safety rather than have a chin wag – and for good measure, because we almost all got killed."

Ellie threw off the bag she'd bravely obtained and knelt down to pull things out of it.

"I'm so sorry, Ellie, baby." Mum apologised. "This is just a big shock."

"It was for me too. I'm only two more minutes ahead of you with the shock. Not to mention the fact that I just almost died three times."

Oh goodness. I shuffle over and hold Ellie tight. "I love you so much." I whisper in her ear. Dad joins in on the hug, and Ellie sobs. She's much braver than I ever would have been.

"We don't have time to recount our stories right now. We need to concentrate on getting out of here." Ellie says with a confidence that impresses me. She's completely right. She pulls vodka out of the bag, matches, torches, and a couple of knives. If all fails, we torch the place.

I turn from looking at what Ellie went to retrieve and see everyone's eyes on me. Great. After everything that just happened, I still have to be the person to tell Ellie about Jackson. Right now, I'd take being outside the room in danger.

-

No. No. This is not the truth. This is not what has happened. I did not go through everything I had just done to be told that our hope; and my boyfriend has been taken by the monsters that tried to kill Kyle and me minutes ago. I am furious. My blood is boiling, and I can't hold it in anymore. I scream. I scream until I have no breath left. I scream to let out all the anger that is bubbling inside me. I scream because I don't know what to do anymore. I scream, and my scream turns to tears.

Finally, I fall to my knees at the window, where I can see Jackson's car seat. Rubeus is upset with my behaviour and runs around me whining. I put my hand on his head, and he nuzzles in, letting me know he'll love me unconditionally. Like Jackson does. Jackson loves me despite all my misgivings. Whenever I do something wrong or out of order, Jackson always forgives me. He's my soul mate.

"Kyle is back with us, and he's going to be ok, Ellie, so don't you worry. We are going to get Jackson back to us too." Steven tries to make me feel better, which I hear, but I don't think anything can make me feel better about this weekend. Ever.

-

We let Ellie have her moment because we all know she needs it. She must be filled to the brim with nervous energy from what she's just been through, and to top it off, she has just discovered that her boyfriend, the wonderful Jackson, is in danger and isn't going to be our saviour. Her scream pains me, but I know she needs to get it out of her system, and I want to hug and hold her, but Kyle's wound is deep, and I am very worried about it.

Using what little medical knowledge I have, I grab the vodka that Ellie brought in the bag and the facecloths from the bathroom. I clean around the wound with the vodka, and Kyle squirms, drifting in and out of his comatose state as I do so.

"I'm so sorry, baby." Steven sobs over his chest as I continue to clean the wound. "Thank you, Shell."

"We are both in the same boat." I say. Although I have Mike, Steven and Jackson, Kyle is my baby boy, and I can't fathom how someone could inflict such horror onto my sunshine.

Once I have cleaned the wound, Steven and I look at each other in horror as we can see just how deep it goes. We need to get him to a hospital, and quick. Unfortunately, the wound doesn't stay clear for long as it continues to bleed. I place a facecloth over it and tighten the belt around his body. He did well to think of that. My clever boy.

"Kyle desperately needs to get to a hospital." Steven declares. "Claire, can I go instead of you? I can try to carry Kyle to the van, and as soon as we get a signal, I'll call the police and drive straight to the hospital."

All

"I don't like the idea of leaving anyone behind but I think it's a good idea if all of us here go in the van." Mike put forward his thoughts to the group. I agreed but I knew Ellie wouldn't be happy leaving knowing that Jackson is here somewhere.

"I know that's the logical choice." She said softly. "But I don't know if I can bring myself to leave without him."

"I completely understand, but if we leave someone or some people behind, then we are leaving more than just Jackson in danger. If all of us leave, at least we are all safe and we can get help for Jackson."

"I know. I understand." Ellie retorted snappily. "But don't expect me to be completely fine with this plan right now. You're expecting me to just jump on board with leaving the person I love in danger with people I now know want to kill us and although when it comes down to it, I will leave, I can't be positive about it. Okay?" Her voiced quivered as she finished.

"Absolutely." I tried to sound understanding. She made me realise what exactly it was we were expecting of her and it wasn't fair. I knew how easy it was to take pain out on those closest to you and Steven and Ellie are admirably rational.

-

"Well, how are we going to do this?" I asked getting impatient. All I wanted to do was get out of here and get help for Jackson but everyone seemed to be hesitant to take lead. Everyone looked from one another in vacant silence. Right, I guess I'll start.

"If we thought there were three of them, I think it's safe to say we only have to deal with two now."

"Why do you say that?" Claire asked instantaneously. I knew she'd be the Spanish inquisition.

"I had a run in with one of them and they fell down the stairs and I think they're dead. Okay?"

"What? Are you serious?"

"No, Claire, I'm lying. Of course I'm serious."

"Why didn't you tell us?" Mum asked moving towards me. She better not be coming for a hug. We've had enough hugs tonight.

"I didn't tell you because you didn't ask how I got on when I came back." I finished and mum wrapped her arms around me. I knew it.

Realising just how snippy I was being, I hugged mum back. Trying not to upset anyone again, I apologised and blamed my attitude on the situation.

"It is a shitty situation." Claire accepted my apology with her agreement, which annoyed me because she should apologise too. She should apologise for being quick with the questions directed at me. Shouldn't she?

Yes.

Maybe.

Probably not. There's my attitude again. Yes, Ellie, ten points for self-awareness.

"Are you alright?" She asked me sincerely and I felt a pang of guilt for being quite so angry at her. I don't like it when she's sincerely nice to me. It puts me on edge. No more so than I am already, I suppose.

"Yes. Thank you. I can tell you the story when we are out of here and all *eight* of us are safe."

"Nine." Mum picked up Rubeus and kissed him. Stop that now.

"Stop that now, mum." Claire shouted. Wow, yes Claire! Now I definitely feel guilty. But she can be a hot mess too sometimes so it doesn't matter.

"It's disgusting when owners do that with their dogs. Rubeus literally licks his bum, mum." I said to show my solidarity with Claire and she winked at me, which I loved. What is wrong with me? Why is Claire's validation anything I care about? Is this night bringing us closer together as a family? Am I thinking poetically? Absolutely not. I shiver out of disgust at how much of a hot mess I am right now and force myself to focus on the matter at hand. Getting out of here.

"Now I'm being serious. How are we going to do this?"

-

"Well if what you say is true and there are only two of them out there; surely the six of us can outsmart the two of them."

"Seven." I added, thrusting Rubeus into view of Graham who so rudely forgot him.

"Seven." He added. I didn't want to say anything in fear of jinxing what I had observed; however, since Kyle's return and us realising there is only two of the figures tormenting us now, we have become slightly more positive as a group. Thinking positively and less panicked.

"Maybe we should leave in groups and signal to the room when it is safe to leave?" I suggest.

"Kyle is losing a lot of blood and I don't know if I'll manage to carry him myself now." Steven added with emptiness in his voice. We were all reaching our capacity of nonsense.

"What if we see where the creepy hidden hallway goes?" Ellie asks walking over to the blocked up cupboard.

"I definitely don't think that's a good idea." I couldn't think of anything more dangerous than to go through something of which we have no idea where it leads or who might be in there. No.

"Maybe these guys will see what happened to their friend when he met me and they'll make a run for it." Ellie further suggested.

"How would we know they'd made a run for it?" Mike asked. "We could be in here for days before anyone comes to help us and these people might call for backup in that time because we don't know for sure that there's only three of them."

Mike was right. We didn't know for sure if there were two, three or twenty. All we could be sure of was that they had Jackson somewhere and he could be as hurt as, or more so than, Kyle.

-

I love it when Mike speaks sense because he always thinks before he opens his mouth. I look at him and smile. That man is perfect. He is my reason for living. As I am staring at my husband, our bubble is popped and we are all dragged back to reality with bashing coming from behind the cupboard.

As the banging worsens, a flurry of panic washes over us all and a rush of adrenaline kicks in.

It appears that these figures knew exactly where the staircase leads and came in from the other side. What are we going to do? We can't outrun them, not with Kyle and we can't hide any longer. Mike and Steven, like clockwork have picked up two chair legs and are stood, coiled and ready just in front of the cupboard door. Mum and dad have moved Kyle away from the centre of the room and Ellie has joined the boys. What do I do? I don't have a place here. I'm not confident enough to stand on the front line and fight but I don't want to waste my energy looking after Kyle when mum has it under control.

Perhaps my job is to plan? Think of a plan, Claire. Think.

Barricade everyone in the bathroom? Probably not the brightest idea. Then we will definitely be surrounded.

Stay and fight the bastards. What if there are more than two? We probably wouldn't see the break of dawn.

What if dad and I can get Kyle down the stairs while Ellie and the boys stay up here? Maybe we can get him to the van and dad can get it started; ready for everyone to make a run for it. That's presuming dad can get the van started. Why didn't we try that when we were in Steven and Kyle's car earlier? We wouldn't have gotten far before banging into Jackson's car and the van, but we didn't know that at the time.

\-

Steven's engineering is working well; whoever they are, they will be tired by the time they get in here. For his safety, Graham and I have pulled Kyle over to the side of the room but now I'm not entirely sure of how safe any of us are. Rubeus is by my side and I think he is starting to get confused at what's going on. My poor little man.

\-

I am so ready for this. I am ready to destroy the absolute pieces of shit. I want them to break down the door. I want them to come at me and my family. I'll swing this leg in their face as hard as I did to their friend.

\-

Graham and Claire have come up with a plan and although I'm not happy about it, I don't think I'll ever be happy with a plan that involves putting any of my babies in danger.

"Ellie." I call her over.

"Mum, I'm fine."

"No, it's not that. I need you to go with Claire and your dad. Cover their backs."

\-

Wow. Mum is trusting me. That's pretty big of her. This is going to work. I can feel it in my bones.

-

I run over and kiss Mike and peck Steven on the cheek. Mum has Rubeus in her arms and she's staying with Mike and Steven. They'll protect her while dad and I carry Kyle to the van.

"Close the door when we leave." I say to mum. "Make it look like no one has left the room in case they get in."

Mum nods. "I love you."

"I love you, mum."

-

As we slide the slats out of the door frame, part of me hopes we will bump into Jackson like I did with Kyle earlier on. I know it's probably not going to happen. The quicker we all get out of here, the quicker we can get help to save Jackson.

All

As the door closes behind me, I have deja-vu, and my heart starts thumping like it did before. I was frozen for a moment before I caught sight of my poor sixty-year-old dad struggling to carry my hefty lump of a brother. I took to the stairs first, listening and looking as hard as possible to make sure I kept my family safe. As we neared the bottom of the stairs, the thudding from the cupboard in the bedroom dulled, and by the time we reached the bottom of the stairs, all we heard was silence. I grabbed Kyle's bedroom door and closed it. I thought it would be safer that way. I'd have the time it took someone to open the door to attack them. I signalled to dad and Claire to wait by the front door before swinging my leg in the darkness of the lounge. After I felt it was clear, I opened the front door and scoped the porch. We are clear. This is too easy.

I leave the door open, so it's easier for everyone to run down the stairs and straight outside to the van.

-

My heart has never raced as much as it is now. I don't know how Ellie has done this twice, and bless dad, he's taking most of Kyle's weight. As we reach the bottom of the stairs, Ellie moves fast and closes the bedroom door. Why did she do that? Did she see something? Most of the floor is pitch black because the moonlight is so faint, but I can only just make out the shapes of the furniture.

Ellie waves at me, and I have no idea what she wants, but luckily dad understands, and we move to the front door with Kyle. Dad gives me a squeeze on the shoulder. That's dad's way of saying how proud he is of one of us. I must look petrified if he's doing it just now.

We then follow Ellie outside and run as fast as possible to the van. Trying to be as quiet as possible, I slide the door open as wide as it can go and shuffle Kyle in. He's starting to stir. He's probably in a lot of pain with neither dad nor I being conscientious of his wound while we have been carrying him. I leave the side door open, and Ellie stands by it with her chair leg above her head. I jump in the front with dad, who is playing with the wires underneath the steering wheel.

"Dad, I'm aware now isn't the time, but why didn't we do this in Steven's car?"

"Steven and Kyle have a fan-dangled computer. Not a car. I could build one of these from scratch, but not modern cars. They don't make them like they used to."

That was the perfect dad answer.

-

I look up at the bedroom we just came from, and I can make out shapes, but I can't see anything else. Hurry up, dad.

Stood, holding Rubeus, I watch outside with my breath held. Please hurry up. The thudding is still going strong, and it sounds as though the figures might be breaking through now.

"I hope you're ready to run, boys." I say, trying to instil confidence.

"Are they there yet?" Mike sounds worryingly alarmed.

"Yes!" They appear. Claire and Graham carrying Kyle with Ellie circling them. I feel sick.

The thudding from the other side of the cupboard abruptly stops.

"Shell." Steven croaks.

I look at the boys and whisper, "Run."

I can see people running down the stairs.

"Dad, I don't mean to stress you out, but they're coming now."

"But we didn't give the signal."

"It looks like they didn't have a choice."

I spot a figure coming out of the darkness from the dining area.

"Ellie!"

"I'm on it!" She shouts, running back to the lodge.

-

Why is Ellie running towards us?

I look over the bannister and see a figure there. They look directly at me, and my heart skips a beat when we lock eyes through their balaclava. I stop halfway down the stairs as Mike and Steven continue running outside. They haven't seen the figure. They run straight out to Ellie. I'm frozen on the spot. The figure moves to the door just behind the boys, slams it shut and locks it, then turns and stares at me.

Kyle's bedroom door opens. Out of it comes a second figure. I hear footsteps behind me, and from the bedroom where we just were, a third figure walks out. They must have been successful in getting through the cupboard.

I'm going to die.

-

"NOO!" I scream at Mike and Steven as they turn around and realise what has happened.

I run straight up to the door and try to open it. It won't budge, so I swing my bat on the lounge window, and it cracks. I swing again and again until Mike and Steven join in, and the window shatters.

"MUM!" I scream in through the window before the three of us jump in.

Where did they go?

Shelley

"Hello, Shelley." The man at the bottom of the stairs menaces. "You have all caused us a bit of a ball ache tonight."

I'm trapped. I wonder if I could throw myself over the bannister without hurting myself. With each thought, the figures are getting closer to me; I need to do something.

"RUN!" I scream to my babies outside, and with the adrenaline of the scream, I jump. I land with a thud at the side of the bannister, and I try to roll towards the sofas. Unfortunately, I'm too late; one of the figures is on top of me. Reaching out, I am able to grab a lamp, and I pummel it down onto the figure's head before I scramble away. I'm screaming, a primal scream that I didn't realise I was capable of, just letting out shrieking wails almost in warning to the figures. Finally, I have made it to the kitchen.

The first thing I feel with my fingers is the thick wooden chopping block, and I grip it and then swing it around with all my might. I've hit a figure. Is it the same one as before? I can't be sure as another is fast approaching me, but I haven't the energy pooled for another swing. I throw the block at them, and they dodge it with a condescending laugh. I let out another scream, and with it, I hop onto the kitchen counter. I've never been so agile. I feel objects, utensils, and food with my hands and throw them at them: every item with a scream. I see their eyes as they reach me and feel a cold sensation in my side. The strength within me, holding my body so steady, disappears instantly, and I slump into the figure. I try to scream, but something stops me. I can't open my mouth. I try again, and some escapes my nose. I have something in my mouth. I'm being dragged upstairs. These aren't nice stairs. I'm not being dragged up the main stairs; I am being dragged up the secret staircase. It must have been in the kitchen somewhere. I hear glass smashing and my babies shouting, screaming for me. I am here, my babies, I am here. I don't want them to come for me. I want them to run. Be safe.

I am dragged into the bedroom, the bedroom that had been our refuge what seemed like an age ago now. There are two figures, and they are pacing. My ears are ringing, but I know they are talking. I can't understand what they're saying, but I know they're not happy. "Where is he?" I think I heard. I try to move, but my body feels like a concrete block of pain, and in shock, I let out a scream, this time managing to rip whatever was on my mouth open with the force. One of the figures turns around and kicks me, then puts more, what sounds like duct tape over my mouth.

"MUM!" I hear Ellie shout. No baby, please, don't come for me! One of the figures grabs me. They pull me up to stand, which makes me shake with pain. Seering through my body, I feel like even my blood is in pain, and I can feel nothing else until I feel a knife on my back. It's sharp point warning me not to move, sitting just below my shoulder blade. The other figure has placed themselves by the wardrobe door, out of sight of whoever may be coming up the staircase. Then I see her. She's holding her bat high above her head when she sees me and stops still. Mike is just behind her. I weep, seeing their faces.

"Come and get her then." The figure with the knife to my back growls.

I shake my head with a whimper to try and warn them not to. They'll be ambushed by the second figure if they do, but the figure digs the knife a little further into my back.

Ellie looks me in the eye, and I try to tell her what the figures are doing. I try to tell her there's a second one waiting to kill her. I try to tell her I have a knife on my back. She grips her bat tightly and gives a quick look to Mike, who nods at her, and they run.

They run towards me. Ellie with her bat seemingly aimed directly at me and Mike with his just above Ellie's head. They know. She understood me. The second figure swings for Ellie, but Mike strikes their head with so much force they rebound off the wall and with that, the figure holding me lets go and runs towards the door. Swinging it open, Steven appears and thrusts his bat into the figure's head. The figures slump in a heap on the ground, and I fall with them. I can't hear anything anymore, only ringing in my ears, but Ellie and Mike and Steven are here. I'll be fine.

All

Dad and I are sat in the front of the van in disbelief at what we are seeing; then we lose sight of everyone, and in silence, we sit staring, set to strike for what seems like hours. Then, finally, we catch a glimpse of movement. Dad drives the van over the path and the grass to the front porch. As he does so, Ellie swings the front door open. She's crying. Oh no.

Mike and Steven are carrying mum out. She's bleeding.

-

"What happened?" Dad shouted, getting out of the van and running to mum.

"They stabbed her." I said while balling my eyes out.

"Steven, drive." Dad commanded before picking mum up from him.

She was unconscious. If they had done that to mum and Kyle, Jackson could be lying in the lodge, bleeding or dead.

I jumped into the side of the van and helped dad and Mike lift mum, in. She laid next to Kyle, and I thought I'd use someone's belt like mum used Kyle's to slow her bleeding down. I noticed then that Kyle was wearing his own belt; it was in his waistband...as well as the one around his wound, so I grabbed it off of him.

"What's happening?" Kyle slurred as I ungraciously whipped his belt off.

"Don't worry, bud. Everything is going to be okay." I assured him, with a slight panic in my voice. Breathe. I need to breathe.

Dad took the belt from me and wrapped it around mum's waist. I looked at the belt around Kyle's waist to help try and replicate what mum did with his wound. It looks like Jackson's belt. Kyle must have picked it up in the lodge somewhere.

Steven starts to reverse away.

"Ellie!" Someone shouts from the lodge.

I look out the side door of the van.

I don't believe it.

It's Jackson.

He has blood all over his face.

Steven stops the van and shouts at him to get in.

"I can't." He says, collapsing to his knees. "Help!"

"Jackson!"

I run out to help him; I'm so glad he's okay. We need to
hurry before they come back and see Jackson is
vulnerable. As I reach him, I see he is really hurt. I try to
pick him up, but I can't. He feels so much heavier than I
thought he would be. It's like he is unable to help at all. I
grab his waistband to try one last time to get him
standing, and I notice that he's not wearing a belt.
Jackson always wears a belt. With my other hand, I take
him by the arms and pull him up with all my might,

throwing his arm around my shoulder. Suddenly I feel the weight from my shoulders disappear as he grabs me, and I feel something cold touch my neck.

"Jackson? What's happening?" I try and squirm away, but Jackson holds me tight.

"Everyone get out of the van now, or I slice Ellie's neck!" Jackson shouts.

"What?" What? I don't understand.

"You heard me."

No. No. "It's you?"

"Yes, it's me."

The belt around Kyle's waist is Jackson's because Jackson is the one who stabbed Kyle. Jackson's car is there because he never intended to leave. He's been here the whole time.

"It's you." I can't believe the person I love has done this to my family and me.

"Keep up. Yes, it's me, you disgusting little fuck. Do you know how long I've been planning this, and you all are ruining it for me?" Jackson whispers in my ear. This isn't Jackson. This can't be Jackson. This isn't the man I love.

"Who are you?" I ask with tears streaming down my face as I watch my family getting out of the van in shock.

"I'm Jackson. Your judge."

"What do you mean? Why are you doing this to us? Jackson, please."

"Jackson, please." He mimics me. "You and your perverse family all deserve to die, and you were the easiest way in to make that happen."

"What?"

"You're an easy, junkie little whore, Ellie."

"So the past eighteen months were all a lie?"

"Yes! Of course, they were. Fuck me. She finally gets it. The most difficult eighteen months of my life. Pretending to love you and your family. The only thing you were good for was a quick shag when I was frustrated at how long it was taking to get you all to come here so my buddies and I could relish over your torture."

"I don't believe you." I screamed.

"Well, you'd better because I'm not lying anymore." Jackson screams back at me. "Why do you think I always fucked you from behind? So I wasn't turned off by your disgusting face."

"I..." I can't.

"Touching you repulsed me."

He isn't lying.

He is going to kill my family and me, and suddenly every piece of the puzzle fits into place. Every argument we'd ever had makes sense. Every suggestion or effort he ever made seemed to have a point. I can't believe what I have done. What I have let loose within my family?

I can't believe I have been so blind and stupid!

I need to save my family.

I have to save my family.

I have to do something.

I have to. I have to. I have to be quick.

Suddenly, I remember I have a knife that I'd put in the waistband of my jeans. Quickly, I prepare; I plant my feet on the ground, take a deep breath, grab the knife, and thrust it into Jackson's stomach. He lets go of me, falling backwards and then to his knees, and I run away from him towards the van.

As Steven drives away, I stare back at Jackson, who has crawled to the seat on the porch and is waving at us. I think I'm in shock and keep staring; my eyes are locked on him until I can't see him or the lodge anymore. We sit in silence on the drive to the nearest town, with mum and Kyle drifting in and out of consciousness. I hope they make it through. I need them to make it. I need them to be okay.

It would be my fault if they died.

Printed in Great Britain
by Amazon

43760136R00189